# Praise for

'Exceptional stories,
stay with you. A true

Huma Qureshi

'The longlist gave such diverse reading pleasures, yet every story, without exception, allowed me to enter worlds which felt carefully realised and full of possibility. As a short-story writer and reader, I don't need much convincing of the special power of the form, but these entries confirmed it once more – and most emphatically!'

Wendy Erskine

'An illuminating and vivid range of stories from an exciting array of new voices already so accomplished in their craft.'

Sharmaine Lovegrove

'I really appreciate the range and ambition on display in these stories. These are writers putting work into voice and craft rather than relying on event alone, and that's what makes their work persist in the mind.'

Chris Power

'One of the best multi-author short-story collections that I have read in recent years. An impressive feat, demonstrating the variety and power of the form.'

Jarred McGinnis

'Testament to the breadth and imagination of a new generation of writers, and the elasticity of the short-story form.'

Anne Meadows

# Brick Lane Bookshop
## New Short Stories 2023

# A BLB Press Publication

Designed, typeset and project-managed by Kate Ellis

First published by BLB Press in 2023
Copyright of the Individual Authors, 2023

ISBN 978-1-9162082-4-7

BLB Press Ltd
Brick Lane Bookshop
166 Brick Lane
London
E1 6RU

www.bricklanebookshop.org

A CIP record for this book is available from the British Library

Printed and bound in Great Britain by Clays Ltd, Elcograf S.p.A.

to opening doors for writers

# Contents

*Foreword*, Denise Jones      ix

*Introduction*, Kate Ellis      xiii

*Kissing in Berlin*, K. Lockwood Jefford      1

*Lots*, Leeor Ohayon      15

*Oyster Shell Ashtray*, Harper Walton      23

*Gybe*, Melanie Carvalho      45

*Second-Hand Smoke*, Chris Wright      55

*The Art of Losing*, Samantha Fern      69

*A Day at the Beach*, Sophia Khan      91

*Entanglement*, David Micklem      105

*Just to You*, Jane Copland      119

*Flight Risk*, Daniel Draper      129

*Ingredients*, Richard Hooton      147

*The Anonymity of a Seaside Town in Winter*,
   Helen Kennedy      157

*Contributors' Bios*      167

*Judges' Bios*      171

*Judges' Quotes*      173

*Writers' Endorsements*      181

*Thanks*      185

# Foreword

## Denise Jones

From 1994–98, when the bookshop was in Whitechapel Road, we ran annual Novel Bursary awards to help new writers take the first step towards a career in the literary world. A literary agent promoted each winner to mainstream publishers, and several became established authors, including Kirstie Speke (*Angel*) and Ben Richards, now a novelist and TV screenwriter with credits including lead writer on *Spooks*, creator/writer of *Party Animals*, *The Fixer*, *Outcasts*, *COBRA* and *Showtrial*, and adaptor of the Robert Galbraith novel *The Cuckoo's Calling*.

Trying to decide what to write in this foreword made me think back five years to the time we decided to resurrect the idea to find and support new writers by creating a short-story competition for Brick Lane Bookshop. I wanted to sponsor the prize through my bookshop, but I never imagined that over those five years we'd receive more than 3,600 stories. I'm grateful to Kate Ellis, who suggested we should go for short stories instead of novels and who has managed the whole process brilliantly since 2019. She chooses prestigious judging panels which each year include an editor, a literary agent and an author: Kit Caless, Emma Paterson, Zoe Gilbert (2019); Sharmaine Lovegrove, Harriet Moore, Chris Power (2020); Kishani Widyaratna, Elise Dillsworth, Wendy Erskine (2021); Anne Meadows, Chris Wellbelove and Huma Qureshi (2022). We're extremely grateful to all of them for giving up their time and for selecting authors who have since been snapped up by other publishers.

I must also thank the writers who submitted their stories, the readers who sifted through all the submissions, the bookshop team and, importantly, this year's judges, Melissa Cox, Kiya Evans and Gurnaik Johal, who had the difficult task of selecting the winners from the excellent longlist.

I'm so proud that sixty new writers have been discovered and published in the five editions of our short-story anthology. We love the fact that the diverse stories in our collections are on sale at Brick Lane Bookshop and in indie bookshops around the country alongside many other accomplished publications by indie presses.

This year it's fantastic that we have partnered with the leading literary agency Mushens Entertainment, who are offering to give feedback to the winners and to advise on how to get an agent. We are also working with the writer development agency Spread the Word, who have kindly offered a package of surprises for the winners. Thanks so much to both organisations.

Finally, huge congratulations to the winner of the 2023 Short Story Prize, to the runners-up, and to each of the twelve writers whose stories are published in this edition of *Brick Lane Bookshop New Short Stories*. It's an amazing and thrilling sample of today's new talent.

Denise Jones
Owner Brick Lane Bookshop Ltd
August 2023

# Introduction

Kate Ellis

Five years ago in Brick Lane Bookshop, Denise Jones and I chatted behind the counter about the possibility of setting up a writing competition. We aimed to connect emerging writers with agents and publishers, to discover excellent short fiction and create a platform on which to celebrate it. That meant we had to figure out how to publish a book, and hope people might want to read it.

Being a writer is a strange thing and it's a total myth that it's a solo endeavour. To improve, connect and to be encouraged, we need other people. On the submission form this year, we added an option to pay forward an entry for writers on a low income. We received many more of these donations than anticipated and each time it made me feel a little fuzzy inside. We'd like to say a giant thank you to all the kind, generous, selfless writers who opted to pay an entry forward.

There seems to be a hunger among new writers for community, support, encouragement and advice about how to get published. So alongside the usual cash prizes, thanks to our sponsors Mushens Entertainment and partners Spread the Word, this year's 1st, 2nd and 3rd prize winners will receive feedback and the opportunity to attend a development meeting, membership to the London Writers Network, and free places on workshops and courses.

Part of the prize, and the publishing process, is having your work copy-edited. To show – and show off – the quality of the original entries, we don't suggest huge structural edits, but we do try to ensure each story is the best it can be on its own terms. Sue Tyley has copy-edited and proofread the anthology since we began, and her work is thoughtful, meticulous and invaluable. Writers always say what a luxury it is to work with her, and how much they've learnt. Her contribution is also vital to me, a novice typesetter; it's Sue's experience and patience that keeps the book production on track and the quality high. (Know that if any of this paragraph survives, there will have been a copy-edit battle about it being superfluous. It's not.)

Since 2019, we've done OK. This is a DIY enterprise, it's funded by a small independent bookshop, and it's run on energy, hope and fast learning. Including this fifth anthology, we've published sixty short stories and sold more than a few books. What started as a project to get my teeth into has become, to quote one previous shortlistee, 'a bit of an institution' – the competition is even listed in the 2024 *Writers' & Artists' Yearbook*. Often now, when I walk into a bookshop, I see the names of Brick Lane longlistees on the shelves and I feel oddly proud that this competition may have been part of their journey.

Each year, the reading and selection process is delightful and difficult and yet I still couldn't say what makes a good short story. Every reader wants something different: connection, escapism, shock, awe, tenderness, familiarity, nostalgia, fantasy, protest, empathy – maybe horror. There's something in here for all those requirements.

Thank you for buying this anthology. I hope you enjoy it.

Kate Ellis
Project Manager Brick Lane Bookshop Short Story Prize
August 2023

# Brick Lane Bookshop

New Short Stories 2023

# Kissing in Berlin

K. Lockwood Jefford

**London, 6th July 2000**

A burlesque night in a Soho club in the mishmash of streets and dead-end alleys west of Wardour. An unmarked door. Narrow cindery concrete steps to a basement. Whiffs of booze-soaked carpet, dodgy plumbing, and overdone eau de cologne. Banquettes in balding burgundy velvet. A corner bar in vinyl and wood veneer. Nipple tassels, fishnet legs and feather boas on the triangular, plinth-like stage.

Celesta, an ex-medical student, is waiting tables – drinks tray in the air, slim, agile and swift in ballet pumps and black second-hand slacks.

Hetty, associate professor of horticulture at a Russell Group university, sits alone in her favourite Vivienne Westwood ensemble, sipping brandy alexanders. Recently split from her girlfriend of five years – they never last longer – she likes the look of the cocktail waitress. Imagines the tight twists and coils of her short fiery-red hair coarse and springy beneath her palm.

Celesta, who is growing her hair in the hope gravity will uncurl it, admires the sleek, straight blue bob of the

1

woman in expensive-looking clothes drinking creamy cocktails on the rocks. She'd like to skim the tip of her tongue along the rim of white foam above those perfectly lipsticked fuchsia lips.

For Celesta, their first kiss, in a black cab racing to Hetty's garden flat in Primrose Hill, tastes of Parma Violets.

Hetty will tell people Celesta – the 'a' swapped by Hetty for the final 'e' of her given name Celeste, adding a syllable, as if she needed embellishment – was performing onstage the night they met, and Celesta won't correct her.

When she moves in with Hetty, Celesta finds an unfamiliar top hanging in her allocated not-quite-half of the wardrobe. A floaty style she doesn't wear. A brand she'd never buy even if she could afford it. It must be yours, Hetty says. Who else could it belong to?

Celesta says no more, just buries it, quietly, in the garden.

> Slide 1
> Plant Blindness
> A human cognitive bias that tends to ignore plant species, including:
> - A view of plants as an inferior life form to animals
> - Not appreciating the unique aesthetic features of plants
> - Not recognising the importance of plant life to the biosphere and human affairs

**London, 6th July 2005**
Celesta and Hetty are having drinks on the terrace of a bar

in Belsize Park. They don't usually go out mid-week, but they're celebrating Hetty's promotion to full professorship. She has been invited to give a keynote address on 'Plant Blindness' the following week at a European symposium on 'Greening Our Cities' hosted by Humboldt University.

Celesta doesn't mention it's also their fifth anniversary. She knows Hetty has forgotten.

The bar is buzzing for a Wednesday. The early-evening news announced that London has won the bid for the 2012 Olympics. Hetty is optimistic it could mean funding opportunities for her East London department.

Next morning Celesta wakes in waves of warmth radiating from the slumbering mass of Hetty beside her, like her own private microclimate. She switches to her side to admire the heft of Hetty, the undulating landscape of her breasts, her chins and necks and rolling folds of flesh. The creases and crevices hers to explore. Hetty's hidden precious places.

Celesta has seen how some people look at Hetty: scorn scribbled across their faces. She always daggers her eyes at them until they drop their gaze. Only she knows how every cubic centimetre of Hetty is required to house her sheer intellectual brilliance, propel the force of her personality.

Hetty got her a job as a researcher – analysing treatment outcome data in a department of psychology. It's dull, dull, dull, but Hetty considers it a perfect option for someone who chose to leave medicine.

Celesta hasn't told Hetty she was kicked out.

She rises before Hetty, drinks a coffee, and smokes a Marlboro Light on the south-facing terrace, admiring the Mexican wave of the hydrangea, from pink to lilac

3

to purple to blue, like so many heads of big hair jostling for prominence. Celesta loves planting, pruning, weeding, watering. Watching things grow. Hetty says it's what she pays the gardener for.

Celesta grew up in a post-war concrete block overlooking a multi-storey car park in Kilburn. A black-and-white life where nothing flourished. For her, the sumptuous space and colour of Hetty's flat – a gift from her parents, who made their money turning bombsites into car parks – is wide-screen epic technicolour.

She surveys the line of Hetty's new hair dye – cornflower blue – beneath her own fingernails. Even in small, private moments, Hetty's presence nudges her.

Celesta knows something is wrong as soon as she walks into the office. People are standing at their desks, looking at each other. Not speaking. Her first thought is someone's died. A celebrity. The Queen. But it isn't that. Bombs going off on the Tube, someone says. No one knows anything for sure. King's Cross is mentioned and Celesta's stomach flips and dives. Hetty takes the Tube via King's Cross. She lunges for the nearest phone to call Hetty's PA who answers immediately. 'She's just come through the door,' he says.

And in that brief, most fleeting of moments, just before relief flows in, Celesta feels an undertow of disappointment.

The following Monday Celesta and Hetty fly from London City Airport to Berlin, Tegel. Celesta always goes to these events with Hetty to proofread, edit and organise her slides. Hetty refers to packing Celesta in her suitcase. As if she's spare underwear.

Slide 2

Causes of Plant Blindness

- Inherent sensory/perceptual bias in humans that prioritises movement, variable colours, threats (i.e. other animals)
- Zoocentric education that misunderstands evolution as linear, with humans ahead, instead of a dynamic, multi-system non-hierarchical process
- Urbanisation that causes a disconnect between cities and nature

**Berlin, 11th – 14th July 2005**

In the taxi to the hotel in Mitte, Celesta is fascinated by the curious overhead pipes in pink and blue everywhere, their twists and bends and almost-knots like an art installation, reminding her of the Lloyd's building, the Pompidou Centre. Hetty tells her Berlin was built on swampland, and the pipes are put up temporarily to carry excess groundwater in a controlled way from building sites to the Spree.

Celesta prefers to think of them as mysterious and abstract.

She has noticed that Hetty – forever seeking out fresh international collaborations and collegiate cliques across academic institutions – is very excited about meeting a professor of landscape architecture from Copenhagen. She spots them talking at the registration event – takes in the Dane's lean, runner-bean body, moss-green dungarees, sun-browned face and straw-coloured dreadlocks. A sunflower. Younger than Celesta imagined. Somewhere between her thirty and Hetty's forty-five. When the sunflower leans in to speak, Hetty tucks a strand of her new blue hair behind an ear, plunges both hands into the pockets of her olive-green Stella McCartney jumpsuit, and nods. Slowly. As if they're sharing a profound truth. And Celesta feels a jab of the jealousy Hetty would say is 'unbecoming'.

When she asks if Hetty has time to explore the city with her, Hetty barely looks up from her signed copy of the book by the Dane.

Celesta takes a U-Bahn to the Botanischer Garten and lingers in the lavish symmetry of the Italian Garden – conical yew trees lined up like a guard of honour either side of a rectangular lawn splashed with foxgloves, delphiniums, and irises. The distant sputter of a motorised lawnmower elicits memories of daisy chains and sun-dappled picnics from a childhood that wasn't hers.

Hetty thinks Celesta, adopted as a baby, should find out who her birth mother is. ('Don't you want to know who you are?')

Celesta says her biological mother is just gametes. Genes. Nothing to do with her identity. She doesn't say that when she accessed her social services file on turning eighteen, she discovered her birth mother doesn't wish ever to have contact. Or that there was a description of her mother's 'short, thick curly hair'.

Sometimes, all Celesta wants is for Hetty to gather her in her firm arms, hold her. Close enough to hear Hetty's heartbeat, soft as a mother's knock on a child's bedroom door.

But this isn't the sort of thing Hetty ever does.

When Hetty phones her own mother, she calls her

'Mummy'. Celesta has to cover her ears.

Walking its streets of flat-fronted buildings in cream, beige, and pastels, terracotta roofs like caps on schoolboys or soldiers, Celesta falls for Berlin. For the broad boulevards intersected by tramlines stretching both ways into the distance, like strands of black linguine. For the couples everywhere, arm in arm, laughing.

Celesta's not sure how relationships are supposed to be, or feel, or how they're supposed to work at all. She knows about leaving, and being left, but not about staying together. Civil partnerships will be legal in the UK later that year but Hetty says she doesn't have time to discuss it. She has a paper to write. A grant application to submit. Hetty is always telling her there's nothing wrong with their relationship as it is. That Celesta is overthinking, overcomplicating things.

> Slide 3
> Greening Our Cities I
> - Epiphytes (mosses, ferns, cacti & orchids, etc.) grow harmlessly on other plants & non-organic structures to reduce humidity
> - Evapotranspiration +/− shade reduces temperatures by 1–4 degrees Celsius. Planting deciduous trees & vines on the west side of buildings is the best way to keep them cool

The express lift shoots Celesta to the revolving restaurant at the top of the Fernsehturm where she orders a glass of Sekt and surveys the city from six hundred feet, dizzied by the fizz, the expanse of the landscape, and going full circle every half hour. She traces a path from the orb-topped domes of the Berliner Dom to Unter den Linden, Brandenburg Gate, and the sweep of the Tiergarten beyond. The vast Volksparks of Humboldthain, Mauerpark, Friedrichshain, Görlitzer, Hasenheide, like scattered offcuts of lime-green lino on her map, from that height are rolling swathes of dark greens and hazy blues. Hetty told her Berlin's post-war evolution involved large-scale manipulation of the landscape. The hilly parks in an otherwise flat city are often giant re-greened heaps of war wreckage.

Bombsites.

The vista tugs at something wistful inside her, something lodged where she can't reach, somewhere behind the curve of her stomach. Maybe not a some-thing but a no-thing. A space, a gap.

In the gift shop, she considers buying Hetty a perfume in a bottle shaped like the Fernsehturm, but buys it for herself instead.

The last night of the symposium there's to be a closing reception at the university for delegates and their partners. Prosecco and canapés will be served in a room with a chandelier suspended from a domed ceiling. French doors onto a stone balcony with a wrought-iron balustrade overlooking Unter den Linden.

Getting ready, Celesta puts on the slash-necked cocktail dress she found in a vintage shop in Prenzlauer Berg – three iridescent rhinestone-studded glass shank buttons across one shoulder caught her eye. The raw-silk fabric, green as rhododendron leaves, complements her fiery-red hair, which never gives up its twists and coils, no matter how long she grows it. She stabs it with hairpins to quell it in a French pleat, and slips into strappy high-heeled sandals. The hem of the dress brushes the backs of her knees as she moves, like a stroke of Hetty's fingernails.

'Sure you want to come?' Hetty says, meticulously layering on blood-red lipstick and regarding Celesta in the mirror. 'It'll be shoptalk, networking.'

When they arrive, Hetty hands her a flute of prosecco, takes one herself, says, 'Oh, I've spotted someone I have to talk to,' and sweeps off into the throng.

Celesta spends most of the party on the balcony with the smokers, enjoying the cooler air and the view of the Staatsoper, the palatial building opposite: all columns and statues on a façade of pink soft as the sponge in Battenberg cake. There's talk about the bombs in London. The Olympics. Who'll be the next chancellor, Gerhardt Schröder, or Angela Merkel.

The conversation begins to tire her. Celesta speaks little German and even though everybody's English is perfect, she knows they'd rather speak German with each other. She is wilting, thirsty for a beer, her sandals cutting into her swollen feet. Hetty, last glimpsed at the centre of a group including the sunflower, is nowhere to be found.

She descends the marble staircase, and starts walking back to the hotel, alone, barefoot, holding her new shoes by their straps.

Slide 4

Greening Our Cities II

- Green ecosystems improve climate & space for social encounters by reducing heat stress, noise, flooding

- Green spaces should be integral to a city's infrastructure yet too often play a secondary role as 'objects' or 'furniture' to add colour & beautify

Celesta wakes on her back with a sense of something heavy sitting on her chest. Breathing hurts. If the airways in a healthy pair of lungs were unravelled and spread out flat on the ground, they'd cover half a tennis court – one of the things Celesta remembers from her brief time at medical school. An image comes to mind: an elegant-looking packet, orange with red lettering – *ERNTE 23*. She likes to smoke local brands in foreign cities.

Hetty shifts in her sleep so the mattress lists like a raft riding a swell. Celesta inhales a whiff of unwashed body infused with last night's eau de parfum. Something citrussy with a hint of spice. Starfishing her arms and legs in the hotel bed that is vast compared to the one they share in London, she feels unrestrained, sprawling, expansive.

In the lemony morning light flowing through the flimsy floor-to-ceiling curtains she sees the cocktail dress over the back of a chair, crumpled but still holding her shape, like a limbless, headless drunk. She creeps on the heels of her sore feet to lift the dress by its shoulders. One of the buttons is missing – the dark almond shape of the empty hole like one of Hetty's eyes, her let's-have-sex-now eyes.

A flashback to last night.

A bar next to the Spree. A raucous, boozy crowd drinking beer from large jugs served by a slim-hipped girl. A girl who, when she takes Celesta's order, compliments her dress. Tells her the German for button is *der Knopf*. A girl whose fingers not only touch but linger on Celesta's forearm when she brings her beer. Slim hips and narrow shoulders. Not much to grab onto when they finally slide the lock on the stall in the *Damen*, but her nipples are pert and proud and hard as frozen berries. Gratifying to pinch and roll.

She shivers, reliving the kiss that got deeper, tasting the hot sticky toffeeness of it, the girl's hips jutting into hers. The clatter of something hitting the floor. She'd assumed it was a hairpin. They'd been dropping like sycamore seedpods all night. But it was the wrong sound for that, more like the crack of balls on a pool table. Glass on tiles.

She checks her watch. Nine thirty. Their flight's not until the evening. Time for a walk. To get coffee and cake to share with Hetty when she wakes up.

Celesta pulls on jogging pants, espadrilles, a hoodie over her head, snatches her Ray-Bans, bum bag, room key.

Her morning-after face stares back at her in the lift mirror. Lopsided. Puffy. Hectic-looking hair. And she'd forgotten the seam on one shoulder of the hoodie is torn and gaping from Hetty's tantrum over the missing slide on evapotranspiration.

Everyone in the hotel lobby is scrubbed and glowing, staff on reception spruce. Pristine. Celesta feels seedy, in need of watering. Hasn't even cleaned her teeth. It's the sort of place where there's a pyramid of polished green apples on the desk, a bouquet of scarlet gladioli on a dais. The sort of place where no one bats an eye.

Celesta steps out the door unaware that six floors above, Hetty has just opened her eyes and ordered coffee from room service. She's also oblivious to Hetty's subsequent phone call to a room in another hotel, Hetty taking a shower, dressing, fixing her make-up, and exiting via the rear lobby.

> Slide 5
> Greening Our Cities III
> City dwellers often resist & common complaints include:
> - Leaves to sweep up
> - Encourages bird droppings
> - Fewer parking spaces

The hotel is on the banks of the Spree and Celesta walks beside it in the sun. Along this stretch are vast tubs of marigolds, glorious in the sunshine. At night they curl inwards and droop, but in the morning light they're open, dew clinging to their petals like tears. It reminds her that, at midday – one o'clock Berlin time – there's a two-minute silence for the victims of the London bombings.

She comes across a small flea market with stalls devoted to GDR memorabilia. Stasi hats and badges. Model Trabant cars in lime green, red, blue, and white. She buys two – blue for Hetty and red for herself – and stuffs one in each pocket of her joggers. They jostle uncomfortably against the tops of her thighs as she walks.

She buys two coffees at a kiosk – milky and sweet for Hetty, black for her – and a slab of Apfelstreuselkuchen the barista packs in a cardboard box.

A clock strikes midday.

Close to the hotel, Celesta sees a yellow Trabant parked in a side street and – pausing to admire its boxy lines –

sees there are two people sitting in the front. Two women. Two women who don't see her because they are kissing. Frantically. Fingers tangling in each other's hair. One has straw-coloured dreadlocks. The other's is smooth, bobbed, and cornflower blue.

A bomb goes off inside her.

She walks on, feeling as if she's fragmenting, shattering, trying to hold onto smithereens of herself that are falling, falling. Her eyes burn and spill, vision blurs. Blinking hard and gritting her back teeth, she grabs one of the hotel's guest bicycles, wedges the coffee and cake box in the front basket, and pedals across a bridge to the opposite bank where she hits cobblestones and the Trabants crash from her pockets. She keeps going towards a church with twin blue spires, vertical, sharp, and still as sentries, dismounts, kicks the bike onto its stand. She upends Hetty's coffee into the gutter, watches the foamy liquid flow away, rips the empty cup into pieces and scatters them. Like anti-confetti. From a perch on a bollard, Celesta sips her cold coffee and scoops up handfuls of cake, shaken to rubble on the ride.

And as the church clock strikes one, Celesta's thoughts turn not to the bombs in London, or to Hetty, or the Danish sunflower. Her thoughts turn to the slim-hipped girl in the bar by the Spree. And she wonders if the girl found her button and, if she did, whether she might be holding it right now, tilting it this way and that to see how the colours shift in the light. Celesta would like this story to end there, but she knows it's too schmaltzy, too neat. Life has never been that way.

She imagines storming back to the hotel room and

confronting Hetty. Declaring that she's sick of Hetty taking her for granted. Diminishing her. Sick of pretence. But even if she could think of clever and sharp and true things to say, she can't quite see herself saying any of them. Or Hetty listening.

If Hetty is even there.

# Lots

Leeor Ohayon

Her bluey-green eyes reflect in the bakery window, her surgical mask really brings them out, eyes like a cat's eye marble, floating amid the display of tray upon tray of hamantashen: poppy seed and prune and something with sprinkles . . . the interior is decorated with crowns and clowns and bunting made to look like ra'ashanim . . . what do the Hasids call it? a grager? a groger? those little Victorian things that rattle around to make noise to blot out his name – Haman's, who cast lots to kill Jews . . . and now instead, once a year, Hasidic Jews put on fez hats, get hammered on an open-top double-decker bus, cruising down Stamford Hill high street, klezmer music blaring out the back, and it's a shame there aren't more Purims in the average year, it's a shame people don't celebrate Second Purims anymore . . . all those locally averted catastrophes turned into mini parties like in Cairo and Rhodes and Ksar el-Kebir – the Purim of the Three Kings – or family-specific deliverances from tragedy, like the Plum Jam Purim or the one with the curtains . . . we could have had a scroll and sweets and dressed up in costume to celebrate the day Dad drove his car into the lamp post by the barber shop – Purim of the Hair's Breadth – or the day Mum got on the 253 with a suitcase because she said she was leaving for good . . . but she was back by dinner with puffy eyes and the table set, couscous soup on the hob . . . Dad slurping his bowl as if nothing had happened – Purim of Bus Stop H – but better than her couscous were the berkuks she made on Purim, boiled in milk and butter and dusted with cinnamon . . . and oh my God, her fijuelas – how could I forget? she'd wrap the thin dough around the fork while it sizzled in the oil, around and around until it came out a fried rose, syrup and sesame seeds on top . . . takes me way back . . . to being a kid, to the thrill around Purim, sifting through the mishloah manot – all that cellophane wrap and gift-basket filler, looking for the good stuff: a packet of Klik, Bisli, Bamba, a Chocolate Log, a small bottle of grape juice for blessing . . . we'd receive them and Dad would open them up, dish the good stuff out into separate baskets to send on, if he caught me rummaging about he'd shout Don't you dare mix things up! he knew who was getting what, who was deserving of the Klik or the Bisli or the Bamba – who got the grape juice for blessing . . . Mum oversaw quality control, she'd stand over the baskets, point to each one, ask: Who for? then she'd open a fresh page in her notepad, scrawl בס״ד in the top right-hand corner, invoke heaven's help onto the page, so to speak, and jot down the things that they still needed to buy . . . when the baskets were ready, Dad would wrap them up with fresh cellophane, curl a gift ribbon with a pair of open scissors, send them out to neighbours and friends, people from synagogue and the community, saved money and trips to the dentist, had everyone gushing how Moshe and A'liza went above and beyond with their mishloah manot . . . he'd chuckle to himself, proud . . . but the best thing about Purim, the absolute best, was the costumes: Power Rangers and Pokémon and Dragon Ball Z . . . until secondary school, after that it was all sexy cats and slutty soldiers, girl gangs in joint costumes, boys too cool for it – came into school wearing trackies – and always, always one prick in a Bin Laden mask or a keffiyeh with a plastic gun . . . Hasidic kids did it right: Queen Esther and Mordehai, and for twins: the Ten Commandments . . . until they hit bar mitzvah, then a fez hat forever after, and I'd come all the way here, to this bakery, just to remember home . . . as if we'd eaten . . . as if we'd made hamantashen at home . . . Mum wouldn't have made hamantashen, she'd be annoyed hearing me call hamantashen, hamantashen, she'd have given me one of those looks and said: oznei haman, with a stress as if I'd misheard – an i-na'al abuk at the end for comic effect . . . she hated it when me and Rach came back from school with their pronunciations: it's brit not bris, say, levaya not lavoya, and if we said I'm shvitzing or Don't be a shnorer – wohohwoh, she'd slap a hand to her cheek, look up to the ceiling and ask, Why are they trying to make my kids like theirs? didn't want us like *them* . . . but also, didn't want us as we *are* – though she wouldn't say that bit out loud, God forbid, tfu tfu tfu . . . she watches in silence as her friends talk about their grandkids, seconds and thirds on the way, Pesach in a four-star hotel in Eilat . . . if pushed she might say: God is the neck – or was it the hand? is it God's hand? . . . the girl with the bluey-green eyes is tapping for my attention . . . her hand on my shoulder, her bluey-green eyes in the bakery window . . . and I know

those eyes . . . of course, I know those eyes . . . Natalie
Yehoshua, Nat Yesh of Asher and Gina from Kyverdale
Road, Margalit's granddaughter with the bluey-green eyes
– eyes like a cat's eye marble . . . because there's that
anecdote, that joke, that someone way back, a great-great-
something-or-other, must've hooked up with a British
officer in Aden – on the hush – which was quite disturbing
because you couldn't tell it without imagining Nat's
grandma Margalit fucking a soldier in the back of a jeep,
not Margalit herself with her pop socks and cardigan, just
her face cut out, superimposed on a sepia-tinted ancestor ...
to be fair, I've heard it before, every Mizrahi, Sephardi
community with a few blond kids in its ranks and a history
of colonial rule will tell you a version of it . . . she comes in
for a hug, pauses, leans forward then stops, sorta swaying
in the air, decides to pat me on my arm instead, rubs her
hand up and down . . . Dan-Dan, she says, Daniel! How are
you? It's been so long . . . How's your mum? How's your
dad? How's Rach – haven't seen her in years . . . I give her
the protocol line: everyone is good and healthy and happy
– no dramas ever – but she's only half listening, she reaches
into her big Fendi bag, pulls out a tickets book, flicks it into
the palm of her hand . . . What're your plans for Purim? she
asks . . . my plans? no plans . . . Purim, haven't celebrated
in years, I say . . . instant regret, told her too much . . . now,
she's smiling, Amazing, she says, I'm organising a Purim
party, La Maschera in Camden Town, complimentary drink
on arrival with wristband, ten till three, come Dan, please?
will be an opportunity for us to catch up, rendezvous,
remember the past! . . . I parrot the words back at her: Purim
party, wristband, rendezvous . . . I don't know what else to

say, don't know what could be worse, swaying awkwardly
on a sticky, glittery floor to an electro-house mix of
Rihanna's *Umbrella*, with all those people from school . . .
all those kids from the suburbs: Barnet and Harrow and
Hertsmere . . . except no longer kids, now fully grown,
actual adults who sound like their parents . . . Becky Green
and Sophie Rose and that lanky one with the attitude . . .
Julie Oppenheim – Goolie Open Hymen, Rafi Silver used
to call her until one day she clapped him straight in the
face, red handprint on his cheek for all of fifth lesson . . .
then there were pricks like Josh Gold, Josh Cohen, lesser
pricks like Danny Haddad, Michael Hajaj – tanned skin,
Hermès belts . . . who has the energy for that? who has the
strength to answer: What are you up to these days? and
Where do you live? Is there a missus Elfassi? What about
kids? Josh Gold grinning in silence because it was always
Oi Fassy, never Elfassi . . . and I'm thinking this, the setting,
the guests, rubbing shoulders, mixing with that lot, and
how did Nat Yesh from Kyverdale Road become a part of
that world? . . . and she looks up at me with those bluey-
green eyes . . . those cat's eye marbles . . . Come, please?
she says, everyone will be there, Sophie Rose always asks
me about you, and Julie Oppenheim as well . . . We'll be
crowning an Esther and Mordehai, she says . . . Weren't
they uncle and niece? I ask, but she just shrugs at me, says,
Honestly, can't wait to tell Mum that I saw Dan Fas on
Stamford Hill high street! . . . How is your mum? I ask . . .
she sighs . . . Not doing well, she says, bed-bound, arthritis,
Parkinson's, a salad of health issues, all downhill after
Asher passed away, this time two years back . . . and I can't
believe it, *Gina*, Nutter of Nat – that's what people called

her behind her back . . . Nat overheard once, burst into tears, had all the girls on the school bus lining up to console her . . . what was it Mum used to say about Gina? . . . called her the thing that blows air into the fireplace . . . she could set the whole place ablaze with her words, big smoker as well, one after the other, wasn't shy of a slanging match at all the wrong times, usually with Rina and her sister Ilana . . . on the synagogue stairs on Kippur, on Simhat Torah during the hakafot – one araq too many in the synagogue kitchen, let it all rip about Rina's husband Shimo'n . . . knew how to open her mouth, and she was always washing that concrete patch she had for a front garden, you'd see her outside with a sponja stick and a bucket, in her house flip-flops, gold anklet studded with turquoise, soapy water running onto the pavement . . . if you walked past and called out Hiya Gina, she'd stop, rest her hand on the stick, head propped up on top, her attention all yours . . . Hello sweetie, Hello darrrrling – Rs rolling into next week . . . Gina . . . Nutter of Nat . . . the thing that blows air into the fireplace . . . she had enough on her plate: Asher with the gambling and the betting and the cheating, apparently . . . she caught him twice with Luna, Rina and Ilana's younger sister – the unmarried one – and if she ever came up in conversation, Gina would make a face like she was about to spit, Gina never forgave her . . . never forgave Asher, didn't forgive Shimo'n of Rina either, he provided the alibis, the ruses, pretended they were at his bakery playing cards in the room at the back . . . Mum always said Gina was miskeena because she'd had a hard life, she carried her mum and all her siblings on her shoulders after they'd kidnapped her brother from the maternity ward, then God gave her a husband like that, that's her lot in this life . . . Mum used to say there are two things in life we don't choose: you don't choose your family and you don't choose your luck, which was her way of saying in life you just sucked it up, God wrote it in the stars . . . maktub . . . we don't know the lots that have been cast up above . . . and now Nat's pleading with me, with those bluey-green eyes, disposable mask at her chin, and I've got no excuse, no business meeting at ten, no dinner reservation with a husband or boyfriend . . . as if I could tell her that anyway, on the high street outside the bakery, so that it can make its way back round to Mum, so she can stand there with her hands in her hair again: Why did you tell her? I told you not to tell her, don't you know Asher and Gina have a big mouth? . . . but Asher is dead and Gina's too ill to care – does it even matter? does any of it matter? and what if I knocked on Mum's door and said: Listen, Mum, I'm not gay anymore, would she put out some treats and put on a costume? would she declare it a Second Purim?

# Oyster Shell Ashtray

Harper Walton

You've always been intensely attracted to people with buzz cuts.

There was the one in Athens, at the loukoumades café, smiling at their friend in between doughy mouthfuls. There was the one at the Hackney bike workshop, their spindly fingers tweaking the spokes of your six-gear. There was the one at your university badminton sessions, who – even in tight-fitting sports gear – was so androgynous you had no idea what they were born with.

You decide it's time to take action. Recently, your friend-with-benefits recommended an app to you.

'It's like a dating app and a social media company had a one-night stand and gave birth to a queer kid who became estranged from them and forged their own identity inspired by punky DIY zine aesthetics,' they pitched.

'Sure,' you said, and waited until they'd gone home before you tapped Download.

You create your profile, using a name you've been trying out recently, one that isn't on your birth certificate or passport. You learn that photos are optional but choose to have one anyway, opting for a pic taken in the yellow-and-red lighting of the Dalston Superstore gender-neutral bathroom. It's your favourite photo of yourself, because when you posted it online a stranger commented *are you a boy or a girl?*

Reading some localised posts, you learn that the app digitises the experience of a newspaper's personal ads section. It's nostalgic but vaguely sad, a virtual platform reanimating the corpse of an obsolete medium.

JUST MOVED TO LONDON
New in town, let's hang out!

LET'S PLAY VIDEO GAMES
Bi gamer seeks IRL friends

TRANSMASC IPA LOVER
Let's grab a pint :)

You envision each post blossoming into several potential outcomes, volatile as if decided by rolling dice. Maybe they'll meet their new best friend, or the love of their life, or a fifty-year-old catfish who drags them to their plastic-sheet-covered basement and revs up their chainsaw.

GOO GOO GA GA
24-year-old sub with oral fixation looking
for milf to feed me with their milkers

PISS ON ME
I want to be your urinal

HORSE GIRL WANTED
Well-hung transfem required for steamy
T4T action. Charming personality desired
but not essential. Enquire within.

You're only allowed six posts a month, so you have to use your words wisely. You opt for self-introduction:

CLAPTON LITERARY QUEER
Open book searching for a voracious reader.
I may not be a bestseller, but I'll turn your
pages. Let's role play as our favourite tropes
and subvert each other's genres.

To your amazement, over the course of the day, your post is rather successful. People react with laughing emojis, love hearts, flames. A stranger pops up, asking if you're free tonight. A beautiful trans girl asks for your WhatsApp and instantly sends you nudes.

For online dating, this is a first. Usually, you barely get any likes or matches, and the people you do connect with often ghost you after a message or two.

You see a post you like and react with virtual laughter, echoing your embodied experience. You beam a smile into the unresponsive atmosphere of your bedroom.

People are sick and looking for buddies to bring them soup and cuddles.

People are starting book clubs spotlighting queer

postcolonial narratives.

People are forming post-punk bands, unable to read music.

People are panicking over the inevitability of death, asking for therapist recommendations.

People are looking for flatmates, looking for rooms to rent, looking for tickets to a sold-out play that reinterprets Joan of Arc as non-binary.

You post again:

### BUZZ-CUT BABES

I have some clippers. You have a scalp that
needs to breathe. I'll give you a free trim
and if we get on, we can rub each other's
peachy fuzz.

You sink into the squishy red sofa in your living room, observing the rain crawling down the window, hyperaware of your phone on the table in front of you and how its face hasn't brightened with notifications.

The raindrops become your closest friends, except they are not the same raindrops that you started staring at an hour ago – in fact you've witnessed a genocide of raindrops, thousands of them suspended in the brief moment between their birth in the clouds and their imminent death on the asphalt in front of your building.

Your phone jolts, your hand springs to it. A message:

@duvet_ripper: *I wish I didn't have a fresh buzz cut so*

*someone could make me have one ugh*

You stare at your phone. It stares back. You look at the window, begging the rain for inspiration. But the downpour has momentarily ceased. You're on your own now.

*How fast does your hair grow?* you reply.

*I like to shave my head every 1-2 weeks*, they write back instantly.

*OK so next time you need it cut, you know who to call.*

*You interested in making a hot scene out of it?*

Your wrist socket loosens, phone grip unsubstantial. You flamingo-hop around the room, brain jelly swimming.

You've always been intensely attracted to people with buzz cuts, but what does that *mean*? What do you want to *do* with that information?

*Yes*, you respond.

\* \* \* \* \*

A month later, you're waiting. They have your address; all they need do is turn up.

Your phone vibrates.

*Here*
(sent 21:38)

No one rings doorbells anymore. Your mind starts walking downstairs, but your soles are frozen to the bathroom tiles.

Disgruntled hair, post-nap eyes, posture that depresses your parents. Your reflection in the mirror looks so nervous you want to slap its cheek.

*Yo*
(sent 21:41)

*Oh shit.* You will your legs to move. You stomp down the industrial metal staircase and heave open the stiff reinforced door.

'Come in,' you say, gesturing inside yourself.

'When you said you lived in a warehouse, you weren't joking.'

'Haha,' you laugh onomatopoeically.

'I was imagining more of a cute, refurbished block of flats with exposed brick and ample loft space. This is *literally* a warehouse.'

'Yeah,' you sigh. The first time you saw it, you'd had the same reaction. The tall façade of corrugated steel, the generic royal-blue border beams, the large sign that read *UNIT 7*. It was hardly the rustic cottage of your dreams.

'Welcome to the living room,' you say, wafting your arms into the empty space. You've seen the sofas, plants and posters hundreds of times. What interests you is the brand-new human being who until a few seconds ago existed only as pixels on a screen and a voice that you invented in your own head.

Their hair is short and dark, sticking up and out like hedgehog spines. Their ears are on the larger side and covered in metal bars like a pin cushion. Their nose is long, their top lip is thick, the bottom one thin. Dark-brown eyes rimmed with thick lashes. The only noticeable make-up on their face is a charcoal-grey eyeshadow. They're wearing a long black leather coat, a black ribbed turtleneck jumper, green cargo pants and black boots you've only ever seen on construction workers. The toe is so worn that some of the steel cap is visible. Their fingers are sausage thick, calloused, and tipped with black polish.

'It's bigger than I expected,' they say. 'How many people live here?' You notice a hint of an accent – German maybe – but don't mention it. People with accents are probably bored of people commenting on them.

'Ten in total.'

'What are they like?' they ask.

'One makes pewter rings in the workshop downstairs, one makes synthesisers out of vegetables.'

'Better than my housemate,' they sigh. 'I asked her what music she's into and she said, "I don't know, I usually just listen to whatever my husband listens to."'

'Does her husband not live with you too?'

'He works in New York, something lucrative. They're doing long distance. I'm always listening out when she has guests in case she's cheating, but unfortunately I haven't heard any noises yet.'

'One of my housemates works for a private consulting firm which specialises in banks,' you say. 'He works from home, and I often see him sitting at the kitchen table on a video call, dressed in a T-shirt and sweatpants, overseeing transfers worth billions of pounds. I asked him once, "Do you ever feel intimidated by the large sums of money?" He said, "Nah, they aren't real. It's just numbers on a screen."'

They look at you. Their eyes are so big and round that consistent contact is uncomfortable to maintain. The room is silent, like someone has borrowed all sound and forgotten to return it.

You want to ask if they fancy taking things to your bedroom, but your mouth has abandoned its post.

'As I was walking here, apart from the skips and pallet boards, the first thing I noticed was the smell of burnt toast,' they say in a monotone voice. You still can't tell whether they're impressed by your unorthodox housing situation or turned off by it.

'Oh yeah, that's the coffee company next door. They roast and grind their beans on site before trucking them off around London. Sometimes I can hear their employees talking through my bedroom wall.'

'What do they talk about?'

'Coffee, mainly.'

'Are all the walls that thin?' they ask.

'You can't sneeze in this house without someone blessing you.'

Silence again. There's so much more you could tell them about the warehouse, or Unit 7 as you now affectionately call it, or Home. You could mention the industrial meat grinder downstairs (a leftover from a former tenant whose autoimmune disease meant they could only consume red meat – apparently their bedroom looked like an abattoir with stainless-steel surfaces and whole pig carcasses on hooks).

You could bring up your two housemates who have different methods of killing the mice they catch in their glue traps. Sometimes at night, when you can't sleep, you imagine being a mouse, little pink toes cemented to an adhesive strip, squeak-squealing up at giants who don't speak your language. You imagine your small brown furry body being held down on a wooden plank by strong, firm hands. A huge silver butcher's cleaver rushing towards you, your head leaving your body. Then the image resets. You're back in the glue trap. But this time you're thrown into a plastic bag and obliterated with a rolling pin, your body reduced to jam.

'Do you mind if I smoke?' your guest asks.

Sometimes just as you're drifting off, you hear a mouse's panicked yelps and know for certain that it has just been caught in the trap outside your bedroom. You can't sleep, frozen in the foetal position, knowing that the mouse will stay there until one of your housemates finds it in the morning and ends its suffering.

'Go for it,' you say.

Your guest takes a pouch of tobacco, filter tips and Rizlas from their black tote bag and rolls. You pick up one of the small yellow Ship-brand matchboxes strewn across the coffee table, light one, and hold it to their cigarette.

Sometimes your housemates forget to check all the trap locations and they discover, weeks later, a small rodent body, starting to rot, which must've slowly starved to death in its final days.

'Thanks,' your guest says, exhaling their smoke almost directly into your face.

You wonder how long internet strangers usually talk before hooking up. Your guest taps their ash into the shell on the table.

'I'd never seen an oyster shell used as an ashtray before

moving to Unit 7,' you find yourself saying. 'Oysters don't really do much in their lives, but we seem to have found plenty of uses for them after death – eating them, harvesting their pearls, making decorative objects from their shells – which depending on how you look at it, I guess, could be their body or their home.'

'One of my vegan friends eats oysters. They don't feel pain because they don't have a nervous system. So, are they even alive?'

'Are you talking about your friend or an oyster?'

They laugh half-heartedly.

'I suppose it depends on what you consider alive,' you say. 'An oyster has some things in common with your vegan friend. They both have a mouth, a stomach, a heart.'

Your guest raises a bleached eyebrow. 'It's not often you can eat the whole of a creature in one go, organs and all,' they say.

You desperately search your mind for more oyster facts. 'Did you know,' you say slowly, pausing for dramatic effect, 'every oyster has both sperm and eggs inside them, and can change sex?'

'Trans icons,' your guest says, smiling earnestly for the first time that day.

You think about the oysters of the world, safe and sound, chilling at the bottom of the ocean. Then being yanked to the surface and ripped open, their precious materials confiscated, their entire bodies slurped into giant mouths. You look at the ashtray, its vulvic curves, its silver sheen, its calcified roughness. Its smooth inner bowl coated with grey dust that will never fully be wiped clean.

You imagine dying. A race of giants prise the skin, the

soft tissue, the meat and organs from your body. They mix it all together, pummelling your matter with a pestle and mortar, drinking the red slop, sighing with satisfaction. They use your spinal cord for a belt buckle, your shinbones for toothpicks, your ribcage for a toast rack. And finally, your hollowed-out skull lives on as their ashtray.

'Can I get some water?' your guest asks.

'Of course, sorry, I should have offered.' You heave your body from the cushion's gentle grasp and rush to the kitchen.

'Do you have any straws?'

'Straws?'

'Yeah, I enjoy drinking through straws.'

'But what about . . . the turtles?'

'Fuck 'em.'

You don't know your guest well enough to tell if they're joking or not. You think about how you used to love straws too, as a kid. Chewing their ends until they were flat. Their fluorescent colours contrasting dark cola. The way their straight bodies refracted in clear lemonade. You remember a short-lived product from your youth. A thick plastic straw containing Nesquik powder, so when you sucked the milk up it magically turned chocolatey. Sometimes you feel nostalgic about single-use plastic. Everything was innocent in 2004.

You imagine an entire field in a far-off country filled with empty Nesquik straws. You imagine the entire world covered in plastic waste, continents of stuff, oceans of it, huge waves crushing you, bringing you peace.

A slurping sound breaks your daze. They smack their lips and let out a satisfied sigh so exaggerated that it seems false.

'So . . . you've had buzz cuts before, right?' you ask.

'Yep.'

'Have you ever given one?'

'Yep.'

'Nice.' You thought they would say more, but they seem completely relaxed, lips pursed, leaning back into the green velvet chair.

'Only once,' they say, eyes suddenly alert. 'Several years ago. To my friend. They had beautiful long curly hair and didn't want to part with it. So they asked if we could do it together. They wanted to move to Taiwan to become a Buddhist monk. They shaved me first. I had hair down to my lower back. I wanted to give it to a charity where they make wigs for cancer patients. I put it in a plastic bag and mailed it to my dad. Once my friend had seen me bald, they felt encouraged to take the plunge. So they closed their eyes and let me shave them. It was weird seeing all their curls on the floor. It was like I just amputated one of their limbs or something.'

Your guest's eyes drift off into space and their face takes on a lost expression.

'Did your friend become a monk in the end?'

'Yes. I haven't seen them since.'

'Oh.'

'To be honest, I was really into them. I'd liked them for years and never said anything.' They swallow as if a morsel of food had made a home in the back of their throat.

'Did . . . did you ever sleep together?'

'Twice,' they say. 'Once just before we shaved each other, and once a few days after.'

You imagine them entangled with their shaggy lover, hoisting dark ropes of hair, then flip a switch in your mind – now two bald creatures writhe on a bed, sweat crystals on bare foreheads.

'Was it different?' you ask. 'Before and after?'

They look at you and smile.

'The funny thing is,' they say, 'my dad lost my bag of hair. It must have got buried under some stuff and he forgot about it. My brother found it recently, and I went home just to see it. It was weird, seeing these remnants of me, from three years ago. My hair's been short ever since that shave. My cut-off hair looked amazingly intact. But it was too late. They don't let you donate hair that old. I unsealed the Ziploc bag, and the smell took me back. The scent of my coconut shampoo was just as strong as before. My hair still smelled like me, even though it was dead.'

'I'm pretty sure hair is always dead, even when it's attached to your head.'

'It's alive at the roots,' they say firmly.

'So you didn't fancy becoming a monk, joining your friend?'

'I seriously considered it for a while. But in the end, no. I wasn't ready to change absolutely everything about my life.'

A pause. The rain skydives, unparachuted.

'What did you do with the bag of your hair?' you ask.

'I was tempted to make a scene out of it, scatter the strands like ashes over a cliff edge or burn them ceremonially on a pyre in the garden. But holding the hair in my hands, thinking back to the day I was shaved, I knew exactly what to do. I packed it in a Jiffy bag and posted it to the monastery in Taiwan.'

You imagine your guest's friend on a thin futon on hardwood, falling asleep holding the bag of hair, the coconut shampoo fragrance sliding gently into their nostrils.

'Would you like to see my room?' you ask.

Your guest nods.

You open your door. To the back of it, you've Blu-tacked a printout of Claude Cahun's 1928 autoportrait. You try to see your room for the first time, through your guest's eyes. The Tibetan prayer flags hanging from the steps to your mezzanine bed. The modest bookshelf (if only they could see your personal library at your parents' house (maybe one day (no, it's way too soon to be thinking about that))).

You flip a switch and the harsh main light dies. You push a button and your room is now bathed in a warm golden fairy glow.

'Feel free to take your shoes off,' you tell your guest, then remember you live in a warehouse, and your floor is cold, hard concrete. The white paint is worn in most places, generating a Rorschach pattern. Today it looks like blood-spatter photos in a crime scene analysis lab if their printer had run out of coloured ink.

You fetch a chair from the dining-room table and place it in the middle of your floor. You locate your clippers on the top of the wooden cupboard you found outside at the end of your street, rain-puckered but still usable. Someone had painted a peacock on the side of it, but now its plumage has all but peeled off. You pick the clippers up, feel their weight in the palm of your left hand.

*Babyliss for Men* it says on one side, a claim that will

be proven wrong tonight.

*Made in China* it says on the other, which has always been true.

You picture yourself giving away all your belongings, letting the lease on your room expire, writing a goodbye letter to your parents, booking a one-way plane ticket to China, googling the factory in which Babyliss hair clippers are made, hitchhiking there, sleeping in the back of strangers' cars, not showering or changing clothes until you arrive at the gates of the manufacturing plant, falling to your knees, begging the factory manager for a job, being stationed on the production line, assembling the products, sweating through your overalls, working seven days a week until you almost faint, locking yourself in the toilet and sleeping in the factory after dark, not speaking the language and relying on one colleague to translate everything for you, becoming good friends with them, crashing on their couch, eating their warm home-cooked meals, realising you finally have a life there, sleeping soundly every night in your new apartment after a job well done, going to work every day with a smile on your face because you have a purpose, being proud of your efforts, pouring all your enthusiasm and energy into every product, ensuring they pass the strictest quality checks, daydreaming about how each one will allow new people to shave their heads and enjoy running their fingers over their unburdened scalp.

'Take off your shirt.'

'Sorry?'

Your guest is standing in the middle of your room, fully clothed except for their firmly planted feet, black-nail-varnished toes clenched. Your floor is covered in a fine film of dust. You can't see your guest's soles, but you are certain that thousands of dead cells are clinging on for dear life.

'Take off your shirt,' they repeat.

'OK.'

You pull your white-and-black-striped top over your head, fold it carefully, and place it on your writing desk.

'You're hot,' your guest says, matter-of-factly.

'Really? Thanks.' You feel a slight chill ripple over your torso. 'What about this?' you ask, fingering the soft, cream-coloured bralette you're wearing today for the first time ever.

'Leave it on,' your guest orders. 'For now.' They look at you with laser-focused intensity. They're much better at maintaining eye contact. 'Sit,' they say, gesturing towards the chair.

'Wait, I didn't think . . .'

'You didn't think you were getting shaved too? You thought it was just going to be me? Have you ever even had a buzz cut before? Have you ever shaved someone else?'

You sit down, silent.

'Good,' your guest says, smiling. They take off their black ribbed turtleneck jumper. Then their baggy navy-blue T-shirt. Their torso is surprisingly muscular, with defined abs and sharp obliques. A sleeper build.

'You're hot.' The words are soft and quiet as they pass through your lips.

'I know.'

They unbuckle their belt and let their cargo pants slip down to their ankles. They carefully step out of them like a snake leaving behind its shed skin. Your eyes are restless but you force them to focus on your guest's face. You drink in their long nose, their uneven lips, which if you're not mistaken, seem to be smirking. They remove their black boxers and stand before you, completely naked. Their legs are fluffy with down and their knees sport purple-grey bruises.

The clippers hum hungrily. Your guest leans over you. Their left nipple is a couple of inches away from your face. In the cool ambient temperature of your room, it is erect, reaching towards your mouth. Your neck is dying to extend itself. You want to hold their nipple between your teeth like a magician's bullet.

But you are rooted to the spot. The seat is unforgiving beneath your glutes. You shift your weight as if holding a full bladder.

The whirring blades approach ever closer. When they finally make contact, you almost gasp. Your guest holds your head securely and guides the clippers from the bottom of your neck to the edge of your hairline. You feel feathers of hair trickle down your bare lower back. Some fall forward in front of your eyes and land on your feet. Every few strokes, your guest blows on you. They brush severed strands away with their rough fingertips. A knot of muscle shifts in their calf when they lean towards you. Your eyes skim the soft domes of their shoulders, and the nest of curls beneath the subtle curve of their belly.

They step back and admire their handiwork.

'Finished?' you ask.

They nod.

You reach out your arms and bring their body to you. You hold them but feel held, as if at the point of contact you switched bodies, and now you are the one towering over them, cradling your shaved head in their hands.

'I'm yours now,' they say.

You don't know how to react. They slip their hands under your arms and haul you from the chair. Lift your bralette over your head and gently kiss your shoulders. Unzip your skirt and pull it to the floor. Slowly peel off your pants and place them on the pile. Take your place in the chair and look up at you, eyes suddenly soft, sparkling with the reflection of your fairy lights.

You run your fingers through their dark hair. It's so sleek that it must have been conditioned this morning. You lean forward and smell it. Coconut. You kiss them on the forehead.

'Ready?'

They nod.

You fire up the clippers and run them gently over their crown. Locks of their hair fall and mix with yours until they are indistinguishable from each other, like a gay couple's sperm in a Petri dish.

Every time the blades touch your guest's head, they sigh softly, almost a whimper. Their toes fan out then curl like ferns in reverse, trapping loose hair in the spaces between. You hold down their ears to reach the trickiest nooks. You prowl around, hunting a three-hundred-and-sixty-degree perspective. Everything appears even and complete.

'Done,' you say proudly. Your guest shakes their body like a dog coming in from the rain. They step to you, pause, look up into your eyes, then fall forward into a hug. You hold each other for a moment, bare skin on bare skin, until the little fragments of hair become violently itchy.

'Shower time,' they say, and you flick your chin down

in agreement. You reach for your shirt, but they grab your wrist. 'We don't need clothes,' they say.

It's late; you reckon all your housemates will be asleep or out partying.

Your door creaks as it opens, hinges thirsty for oil. Your guest feels for you in the encroaching darkness and your fingers interlock. In the living room, you are both hardly more than silhouettes against the moon glow that drifts down from the grimy skylights. A chilly breeze wafts from the two open industrial windows. The cold wraps around your ankles, needles at the pores between your thighs, ossifies your nipples until they are hard and sharp as diamonds.

In the shower room, neither of you turns on the light. You stand under the hot stream of water. It is as if you have ceased to exist, and your state of being is a void filled only with steaming wet black.

Your hands find the body in front of you, not your own but theirs, bumpy gooseflesh smoothing to flat planes of skin. Your bodies lock together in a soapy seal. You are taller than them, but you knew this already. Their lips rest on your collarbone, soft on hard, slick on slick.

With tangy grapefruit gel you eradicate the clingy hairs from each other's shoulders. You murder hundreds of tiny bubbles on your guest's back. Running your fingers over their head, you enjoy the subtle roughness of the stubble, the ease with which your whole hand can travel the length of their scalp.

They rub your shaved head and it sinks in: you have no hair anymore. You smile an invisible smile in the dark, but your guest seems to notice, as they reach their fingers up to

41

the corners of your mouth, tracing the outline as it widens.

Time has ceased to exist. In the waterlogged murk, you are simply two bodies, twins in a womb. One of you turns off the shower, you can't tell which – maybe you reach for it at the same time and pull the lever hand on hand. You birth yourselves into the bathroom, pushing through the veil of the plastic curtain. Two black shapes are trapped in the mirror above the sink. Flicking the light switch sets them free. The harshness of the industrial strip lighting blinds you.

Two ghosts. It takes you a second to tell you and your guest apart. As your eyes acclimatise, you notice the incongruence between your bodies, your faces. The same paint on different canvases, now scraped off.

The powerful overhead beam casts severe shadows under your eyes and cheekbones. Your guest's ribcage sculpts into their skin. Your baldness reveals the rotundity of your skull, offset by the angles of your jawline. Your eyes have sunk into their sockets.

*Remember you must die.*

Glancing at your guest, you wonder what they're thinking or feeling. Their face is neutral, betraying no emotion. But your insides are boiling.

*Remember you must die.*

It may be in sixty years, or tomorrow. The world will keep moving. But for you, everything will disappear. All your memories, all your plans for the future.

*Remember you must die.*

No heaven, no hell, no afterlife. You will be nothing at all. You will cease to exist. You won't think anything anymore. You won't feel. You will simply be gone.

Being nothing.
Not being.


But you are not dead yet. And you aren't alone, either. There is someone right next to you. You can reach out and touch them, if you want.

Your mind is racing. But that means it's still working.

You're terrified. You can tell because your blood is pumping faster.

Because you have a heart inside you.

Touch your chest or your neck or your wrist.

It is beating right now.

# Gybe

Melanie Carvalho

A good technical sail, Laila's dad said. It's easy to move fast in high winds, but to get the boat moving in the right direction, with no wind to speak of, is a true challenge. You can learn a lot here. Then one day, I'll take you out to sea.

The boat drifted along the side of the dock, bordered by blocks of flats and city high-rises set against a grey sky. There was no wind to speak of. Let the sails full out, her dad called, his eyes closed, already at sea, palm trees lining imaginary shores. He was settled in the stern, his hand resting on the tiller. Laila sat forward, handling the jib, the brown pooled water in the bottom of the hull leaking through the cracks of her battered hi-tops. They had driven up from Bexleyheath to Surrey Docks that morning, as they had done every Sunday since the new watersports centre opened. A man with greasy brown hair and a beard that covered half his face stood on the dockside, allocating dinghies.

I am training her to be my crew, her dad shouted to those setting out around them, into the still, black water. So I can relax and drink my gin and tonic into the sunset.

On the way up, Laila would notice the people becoming browner and feel herself relax, her body softening against the leatherette seat. Last night, Laila's parents had come back early from their dinner party. Her mum was shaking her head. Your father plays nice, doesn't want to cause a fuss, but I won't stand for it. When they start, I get up, I put my coat on, I say, we're leaving.

Why do you stay friends with them? Laila had asked her dad on the drive up that morning.

If I did not have racist friends, then I would not have any friends, he replied evenly, white smoke streaming from the side of his mouth, his rollie moving from hand to lips as he steered and changed gear, through Welling then Eltham then Greenwich, to a place that seemed less complicated to navigate.

The regenerated dock was surrounded by high white walls running twenty feet up, along the top of which ran a black-painted balustrade, all the way around. Families were appearing above, stopping to peer down at the hesitant, fractured flotilla. On the far side, a group of teenage boys, about Laila's age, seventeen or so, were laughing and pushing each other, and drinking from cans of beer, though it was only 11 a.m. Immediately overhead, a little girl stuck her head between the railings and looked down at them. She was wearing a pink puffa jacket and her long black plaits swung down towards them like ropes. Laila smiled up at her, and she smiled back and waved. Her mother noticed her daughter then and tugged her hood causing the child to crack her head momentarily against the cast iron and cry out. Her mother responded sharply in a language Laila didn't know, Bengali perhaps, or Urdu.

There was only one other brown girl at Laila's school, and they made sure not to be friends. When the other kids made jokes about Cadbury's Fruit and Nut, Laila pretended not to hear, or understand. She actually didn't understand, but she understood that they were about her and Nina Patel, and that they were not funny, to them, at least.

The boat was barely moving. A good technical sail, her dad repeated. He was an engineer. He loved to problem-solve, to think about forces, and balances, and how to channel the little you're given to your best advantage. He liked calm waters, smooth sailing.

But Laila loved to race, to go fast, snagging gusts of wind that would occasionally blow up with sails pulled in tight, tilting the boat on its edge. She would sit high up on the opposite side, controlling the wind, the water, the sun and the stars, channelling everything she'd been given to her best advantage.

It is in your blood, her dad told her. Our ancestors were fishermen, off the south-west coast of India.

But Uncle João says we were *kshatriya*, warrior caste, she replied.

Your uncle is a snob, he said. We were fisherfolk.

The first time they came, they had to do an induction and a capsize drill before they went out. The bearded, greasy-haired man sat with them in the boat, and shouted things like Ready to gybe! And showed them how to duck when you gybed, to stop the boom from crashing into your head when it swung across, and to make sure the centreboard was down, so that you didn't capsize, but then he got out before they did it on purpose, for real. She had to stand with a foot on the edge and let the sail drop out, and lean forward into

47

the water, and even though she knew what was coming, had done it to herself, in fact, it was still shocking when the boat tipped past the point of no return, and she fell into the water headfirst, in a kind of somersault. She plummeted into the icy black water, and shot under further than she thought she would with the weight of her waterproofs. She had stayed there for a moment, in the freezing depths, before coming to, and kicking her way to the surface.

More people were appearing above. The new shopping centre next to the dock was open on a Sunday now, and it drew them out of the local estates and luxury waterside apartments towards it. Laila's mum didn't approve. She was at Mass right now, but this was Laila and her dad's time for reflection. Nothing but grey sky above, and black water below.

Your mother will be saying her prayers for us, her dad said, laughing. Do not let them capsize, oh Lord, she will be saying.

Laila laughed. Not at this water temperature, oh Lord, she said, but part of her had enjoyed that moment in the cold black water; her own power when she kept hold of the mainsheet and kicked hard, then swam around, climbed onto the centreboard and heaved the boat up and herself over the side. Everyone on the dock had cheered, and she had felt triumphant.

Do you want to take the tiller for a bit? her dad asked. I'll be your crew. Then I can relax.

They shifted positions carefully, Laila moving back first, and taking the mainsheet and tiller, while her dad crept forward, keeping his body low. The clouds were shifting, and the sky was turning blue, but the water was still dark, reflecting the city skyscrapers around them, which glinted in the emerging sunlight. The boys on the far side were shouting, smoking, kicking a ball around. The other Sunday strollers were giving them a wide berth. There was a forcefield around them that extended out across the water, all the way to Laila and her dad.

Nina Patel got it worse than her, because she was proper brown, her skin the shade of the burnt sienna oil paint Laila had just begun to use in Art. Laila's mum was white. Her dad had met her at a party not long after coming over from India. She was pretending to smoke a cigarette, he said. What a waste! I took it off her and smoked it properly.

Laila settled into the stern of the boat, but did not rest easy as her dad did. She sat upright, holding the mainsheet, with the tiller bent across her lap, watching the water, feeling the slight breeze on her skin. The dock was a square, or a rectangle, actually, and they had completed two sides of it, nearly. There was one short wall, and then a long one back to base. The boat was moving so slowly that they would probably only do the one circuit before getting out and having a cup of tea and her dad a cigarette that she would roll in his rolling machine, before driving home for Sunday lunch. The rollie would come out perfectly: a delicate, papery white cylinder. She would hold it to her nose, like her dad did, before passing it to him, and lighting it. Blow smoke rings Dad, she would say, and he would inhale deeply, then pop his lips like a fish, and circles of white mist would waft gently towards her. She would crinkle her nose up as if in distaste but she liked the smell really.

They were approaching the opposite wall, where the

49

boys were gathered. There were more of them than she had first thought, maybe nine or ten. They were all white, except one, who was mixed, with pale brown skin like hers, his soft curled hair gelled and slicked back like the others. She looked behind her and could see the little girl becoming smaller. A pink dot. She turned back around. The boys' shouts and cries were becoming clearer. She heard the tallest one shout Shut up Warren you slag, and a stocky one respond Fuck off Gav you prick, and she began to tingle inside, a warning sensation.

Her dad smiled at her, as if to say, don't worry, and instead of reassurance, she felt pity, for him, for his belief in people; then shame for them both for the complex mind manoeuvres they had to constantly perform, unknown to everyone, including themselves, sometimes.

She felt sorry for Nina Patel, but she wasn't going to be friends with her. Not that Nina wanted to be friends with her either: she had Sheila Waterson, whose mum was old and so she had come out funny-looking and was still only four foot nine even now, in sixth form. Laila had Tina Santoro, who was 'alternative', and didn't care what the sheep thought. Tina powdered her face as white as possible, and painted her lips dark red, or even black, and Laila only ever borrowed the lipstick.

She gripped the tiller tightly, and wriggled her cramping toes inside her trainers. She was trying to focus on the air, and the water, and the elements external to her, but her internal elements were taking over, and the whooshing in her ears, and the currents coursing through her body, were harder to control. Through the whooshing and the shouting she could just about hear her dad saying, We are nearing the corner Laila, you need to turn the boat, to come around.

The wall to her left was sheer and high, like castle ramparts, huge limestone bricks sandblasted white in the dock regeneration, the freshly painted glossy black balustrade in stark contrast. The boys were directly overhead now, leaning over, silhouetted against the sky, becoming part of the railings, and she could see the wall in front too, and that they would soon be cornered. Her father was still speaking, telling her something, more urgently now, but she could only hear the boys above, laughing, shouting. Fuck off Pakis, fuck off.

The tingling turned ice cold, and she could no longer feel her toes, her hands, the roughness of the ropes, and so she held on tighter to the tiller and the mainsheet, and shot a look back towards the family who were now far behind them, the pink dot moving away from the dock in the opposite direction, as if repelled. She turned back around and saw the boys leaning over still, the brown boy more than the others, yelling louder than the others. The sound in her ears was enormous. Fuck off Pakis, fuck off.

She needed to drown them out, to prevent her dad from hearing what he had already heard, or pretend to him that she hadn't heard it herself, that he didn't need to protect her, to show him that she was still sailing, that she was in control. She shouted, Ready to gybe!

The boys erupted with laughter. She swung the tiller hard and pulled on the mainsheet and the boom came smashing across, drowning their cries out, and the boat swung around, and began to move away from the boys, who were still shouting, but the words were less distinct. They reverberated nevertheless.

51

Her dad said Well done Laila, it is hard to turn the boat around in these conditions, with barely any wind, and she felt furious at him, for not flinching, not reacting, pretending that what was happening, wasn't happening; but it was still happening, and she swung the tiller again, and again, with force, and the boom smashed back and forth, again and again, drowning out the noise in her head and outside in the air, those words being carried on the nonexistent wind, into that vacuum, until the boat turned all the way back around to face the boys.

They looked at her and laughed, but quieter now. The tall one put a hand on the stocky one's shoulder and said something, and the stocky one pushed his hand off, but he turned and began to stride away, his face red, and the others followed, still shouting and laughing, except for the brown boy, who threw a cigarette butt as he left, eyes flashing, mouth shaping those same sharp, terrible words, words which, each time, every time, ripped through the fabric of the moment, and left it hanging.

The orange light of the spark settled on the water's surface, then went out.

They floated there for a while, the boat rocking gently from side to side.

Her dad leaned towards her and touched her knee. You see, it is in your blood. He sat back and closed his eyes against an imaginary sunset. She looked at him but she couldn't see him. Could no longer hear him. She could only hear the blood rushing in her ears. Turning everything red.

She felt bad for Nina Patel but she wasn't going to be friends with her, no way.

Letting go of the tiller, she stood up against the now

clear blue sky and let the mainsheet full out. There was no wind to speak of. It was completely still. She put her foot up on the edge, and her dad opened his eyes and looked up at her. She looked away, into the bright blue above the balustrade, above the glinting high-rises that surrounded them. The light shone in her eyes. She saw herself leaning out into that blue, pushing her cracked hi-top trainers down on the worn fibreglass edge, the dinghy beginning to tilt, slowly at first, then, as the water rushed in, tipping, suddenly, until it was at right angles, then over, and herself and her dad somersaulting forward, through the light and into the freezing, unfathomable black water, drowning everything out.

# Second-Hand Smoke

Chris Wright

The half-dead building that held on to Dad's shop in the late 80s was a wonderland for kids like us; all dusty rooms, heavy doors and secret staircases, its thick walls doing their best to shelter us from the worst of The Troubles raging around us. It was a converted dry goods warehouse in Talbot Street, Belfast, built in the early 1900s to try and revive an area better known for the procurement of 'social evils', namely whiskey and whores, despite it being in the shadow of the cathedral, or perhaps because of it. It was one of many short-lived conversions spread out over the century. Warehouse, newspaper, bombsite, clothes shop, bombsite, gym, nightclub, scene of a brutal sectarian murder. Then, three months after a man's blood was sprayed up the wall in a volley of shots, peace finally graced the streets in its translucent form. Once again, hope transformed the building's weary insides into something more: high-end restaurants, apartments, offices, and an artisan coffee shop, built on top of the gravelly car park – where me and Bill used to kick a ball around – and tacked onto the side of the old building, its new walls a dated terracotta to blend in with the old walls next door. Seeing it now, that scarred façade of new and old, puts me in mind of a skin graft, a facsimile of the old that stands out more in its attempt at similarity.

Back then, it was a magical place for me and my brother to play on a weekend. Dad was still alive, and his clothes shop was hanging on for dear life on the ground floor, only surviving because of the lack of chain stores in Belfast at the time due to the risk of an IRA bomb scattering your inventory across the street amongst the body parts of your employees.

My granda owned the building and loved to remind Dad of it along with the fact that he was lucky to be running the family business. His older brother might have been the one to take the reins, if they had still been on speaking terms. Instead, my uncle was just another name on a long list of people my granda refused to speak to. A list which included his own brother, an ex-member of the B-Specials like my grandfather, and my rarely spoken of uncle, who had moved to America, then converted to Catholicism on his deathbed. As if that wasn't enough, he had the sheer audacity to survive and maintain his newfound allegiance to the corrupt papish dogma.

All of that was just noise to us. We were more interested in the now, and there was always something to conquer our imaginations in that place. The week before, it had been the thrall of the regalia room, hidden in the back of the shop behind a steel door like you'd find in a bank, that really took hold of us. This was where the sashes were made for the Marching Season, each one a resplendent orange with gleaming buckles and badges that flashed white hot in the glare of a fluorescent bulb. Seeing such powerful symbols stripped down to their component parts only served to heighten the thrill and majesty. Spool upon spool of orange and purple cloth. Great silver letters, *LOL* — which for us stood for Loyal Orange Lodge, long before that initialism became something flippant and light you sent to your friends — followed by the lodge number on thick pins. There were even special rings where the stone spun around to reveal a compass and square so you could show proof of membership to your other secret brothers in the Masonic.

The regalia room belonged to my granda – the one part of the business he wasn't prepared to hand over to his second son – and was strictly off limits, which made it virtually irresistible. We had crept down the back stairs from the first-floor stockroom, prised open the massive door and slipped unnoticed into this hidden world at the back of the shop to scour it for the source of its power.

Rows of ageing sewing machines with worn foot pedals sat idle, the room still vaguely warm from their weekday toil. Nimble fingers putting together the sashes the whole Lodge wore as they walked. Dad was always out in front, his face burning with pride as he led the men through the streets he grew up in, like it might scare the bad men away. He carried the silver mace that was too heavy for me and my brother to lift, even together, curling it as he marched, the metal gleaming in the sun as it rose and fell in time with his feet. We'd be running alongside, wearing our own fake sashes, and beating plastic drums, Mum dragging behind us, uninterested in the garishness of ceremony. We were close enough that the thump of the bass drum resonated within our chests, the squeal of the flute so strong and loud the whole world must have heard our song. It was a joy that easily captured young hearts. An acontextual display of colour and sound wrapped up in the misted scent of pride and tradition. We took the feelings of others and made them our own. It would be many years before we understood what it meant.

That Saturday morning, we climbed and hid in the stockroom racks. It was eerily quiet, and we were sure to keep it that way to try and avoid the rollicking we got the week before when Dad caught us wrapping each other in orange ribbon in the place we weren't allowed. Then Deirdre, the woman who helped with the admin, had come up to check some stock and had no idea we were hiding on the top shelf of a tall rack. She knocked over some men's suit jackets and swore loudly, and Bill shouted, 'Language, Timothy,' like the woman on the TV, and she jumped and swore again, and we laughed and laughed until our bellies hurt.

Mum smirked in the background as Dad told us off again and made us apologise. Mum never liked Deirdre and afterwards she made us strong, sweet tea and let us have our fill of Ginger Nuts, while her and Dad continued to argue in harsh whispers. Mum said Deirdre was useless and was only there because Granda was shagging her, which I thought had something to do with carpets. Dad was in a foul mood after that, so we made sure to keep out of trouble to avoid another guldering or clip round the ear. It was becoming a full-time job, evading his wrath, so, instead of messing around like usual, we found a quiet spot to play with a tattered deck of Tank Top Trumps I kept in my pocket.

Bill and I sat facing each other, each cradled in the splayed curve of the stockroom windowsill. Bill seemed reluctant and his attention drifted outside often. I watched him closely, a niggling fear keeping my attention from the mannequin parts, stacked lazily in the corner like a mass grave, that made the room feel both dead and alive at the same time.

Challenger. Weight, sixty-two and a half.

Bill ignored me, his eyes still locked on the streets beneath us. His card lowered as his grip relaxed. I could see it. The M109. Only twenty-nine tonnes. I'd already won.

Challenger. Weight, sixty-two and a half, I repeated slowly.

Still nothing. His eyes moved as if following something.

Bill!

What? he said, head snapping back to me.

Challenger. Weight. Sixty-two and a half tonnes.

He threw his card down without looking, his gaze returning to the window.

You not playin' no more?

I'm watchin' the robot, he said without even a hint of humour in his voice.

What robot? I asked, setting down my cards and craning my neck to see from his point of view. Where?

He pointed into the distance.

Over there. It's about to go behind the cathedral.

I slumped back down and lifted my cards, tutting as I did.

I thought you meant a real robot. That's just bomb disposal. Sure, it's just a big arm on wheels.

It looks like Johnny 5. Are you saying Johnny 5 wasn't

59

a robot?

He could talk.

I don't care. I want to watch it.

Sure, it's only just at the car now. It'll be a while before it does the control 'splosion. We've time to finish the game.

Nah, 's OK. You win.

But . . .

I was about to start a whinge that I knew would bring on a fight when Mum appeared from behind a rack. One look out the window and her body locked, and she took a deep breath.

Jesus Christ, would ya get away from thon window. If that blows there'll be glass everywhere. I'll be picking it out yer clothes for a week. Now, go on. Back downstairs where I can keep an eye on ya.

Mu-um, we replied in unison.

The rest of the morning passed awkwardly. The bomb scare had emptied the shop. Dad made his calls, Deirdre worked on the books, Mum nipping across every so often to glance over her shoulder. When she wasn't checking Deirdre's work, Mum printed out figures on a long paper snake, feeding out from the lump of a printer, its line-by-line screech tugging at the quiet. Me and Bill sat on the floor, tearing the dotted borders from the sides of the pages, collecting them in a pile between us. I was happy because I was helping. Bill just enjoyed the ripping.

The deep thud of a controlled explosion shook the hanging jackets. A flash of frustration crossed Bill's face when he realised the windows were still intact. The bomb must've been a dud.

When the cordon reopened, and the police and army

cleared off, we went into the town for lunch — to the place with the nice chips and the elderly waitress with drawn-on eyebrows that made her look like an angry scarecrow, on the other side of the army gates that ringed the city centre.

There was a buzz as we approached the search box, built originally of iron and covered with Perspex when they realised the war wouldn't be over by Christmas. It looked like a prison cell, yet nothing felt as safe to us as walking through the checkpoint, where brave men stood, ready to save us when the bad men struck. I never even considered that it could feel any other way to be searched by burly men with camo gear and guns. That day there was even a black soldier, cradling what Bill told me was an L1-A1 SLR — or self-loading rifle. Bill had been keeping an eye out for the new SA-80 that he told me had just been brought into service.

As we waited in the queue to be searched there was a bit of a kerfuffle when someone called the soldier searching them a 'black bastard' even though he was white. Two more men in green togs came from nowhere and dragged the man off by the scruff of the neck.

Must be one of the bad men, I thought. Why else would anyone be cheeky to a soldier with a gun? I couldn't even be cheeky to my mum and all she had was a wooden spoon with a sad face drawn on it.

The waitress dropped sausage, beans and chips down in front of me. Everyone got something but Dad, who sucked on a cigarette intently, staring out of the window, turning occasionally to blow smoke over our heads as if that might protect us from it. There was something hypnotic about the way he smoked; long, thoughtful drags, the sound thick and peppered with the snaps of cheap tobacco as he drew blue smoke into his lungs, returning it to the world, white and ghostlike. His cigarette smelled so good when first lit yet would become acrid and cloying after a few deep draws, much like that nighttime medicated smell that clung to him, the one I had recently noticed creeping around him earlier and earlier in the day. It was on days like this, when the smell came early and he ate little and said even less, we learned the hard way to keep quiet and out of his road.

Mum ate little of her lunch as usual, instead taking more pleasure in her coffee. She would lift the cup slowly, preparing her lips long before it reached them. She sipped the piping-hot liquid, seconds after the waitress set it in front of her. I once tried to drink hot tea as quick, but it burnt the inside of my mouth. It was sore for a week. I just couldn't understand it. Surely, the inside of our mouths must be the same, yet hers seemed impervious. You must get used to pain, I thought.

My attention turned from the sad look that overcame her every once in a while to the window, looking out to try and see what Dad was staring at. It was just people going about their day. People shopping. Buses passing. Policemen and policewomen patrolling, gripping tight to more guns that scared the bad men away.

Some days I wanted the bad men to come, like Dad said they would, one day. I'd watch the police and the army fire their rifles and take them out, one at a time, like in the films. Maybe one of the soldiers would get into trouble and drop his gun to clamp his hands over a bullet wound and I'd run out and lift it and shoot it from one hand, holding off the bad men until backup arrived.

It was the least I could do.

Dad stubbed out his cigarette. Shift, he said, giving Bill a nudge to let him out of the booth. He reached in his back pocket, pulled out his wallet, and made his way to her with the drawn-on eyebrows who was perched on a stool by the door, filing her talons. I always wanted him to slap a big note on the table and walk away, like they do in the films, but he never did.

Finish up, boys, Mum said, emptying the speckled dregs of her coffee into her mouth. Bill and I raced to finish our drinks and, by the time we took the last powdery gulps of strawberry milkshake and put on our winter coats, Dad was lighting up another cigarette outside the front door, glancing up and down the street, foot tapping impatiently.

That night, after a dinner of mince done in OXO cubes, huge onion chunks, and overcooked spaghetti — Mum called it spaghetti bolognese despite it never having been so much as threatened with a tomato — we bathed and then dried out in front of the fire, trying to outwit each other at *Catchphrase* on the TV.

Mr Chips was under a blanket, big black boots sticking out one end, a proper English bobby's helmet poking out the other.

Undercover cop, I shouted first. Mum cheered when it turned out to be the right answer. A police message flashed across the screen, cutting off the laughter like the switching-off of a stereo.

POLICE MESSAGE
A DEVICE HAS EXPLODED IN DONEGALL
STREET, BELFAST. POLICE ARE REQUESTING ALL
KEYHOLDERS IN THE AREA TO RETURN AND
CHECK THEIR PREMISES.

Ah, fer fuck's sake, Dad said, throwing his cigarette into the ashtray, it smoking away long after he had made it to the car. It usually took him a couple of hours, while Mum's fingers tapped, and her tone sharpened. It would inevitably turn out to be nothing, but I hated it when he had to go like that. He never looked scared even though he could be walking into a bomb, but I sure was. More so now I knew that if the bad men could take my friend Peter's dad away, they could take mine.

It was the following weekend when there was no message and an actual bomb. We were roused from our beds in the middle of the night and bundled half sleeping into the car. When we arrived at the shop, the walls were lit up blue and red like a school disco. Soldiers marched along the fluttering tape, policemen and firemen scurrying like ants inside the cordon. Great flames licked from the window frames where me and my brother had sat and played Top Trumps. Glass littered the street, crunching under firemen's boots as they wrestled with wayward hoses.

Dad lifted the tape and stepped under like he was one of them. He lit up orange, then red, then blue, the sequence repeating over and over again. As he talked to the policemen, he mirrored their stance – legs wide, arms folded, rod-straight back – and nodded as the situation was explained to him as if it wasn't obvious.

Dad made his way back towards us, stopping to take one last look at his life, rippled in flame and black smoke, funnelling into the cloudy night sky. He wiped his eyes, and I knew it wasn't the smoke that was bothering him.

It was just another horrible event, talked about around us but never to us. I had to piece together overheard conversations during the next few weeks before I managed to find out that the bad men had slipped a firebomb — a camera flash attached to an alarm clock and packed into a cassette box with flammable materials; when the timer went, the flash bulb went off, igniting ground match heads which, in turn, would ignite a container of lighter fuel, starting a small but fast-moving fire — between pairs of stonewashed jeans at the back of the shop.

Apparently stopping Dad selling suits to old men would help the bad men win their war. It was a scary thought, them winning, because Dad said if they did, they'd march down our street, line us up against a wall and shoot us all dead.

Not long after the shop burned down, we were watching the news and some guy who looked like a farmer was shooting and lobbing grenades at the funeral of some bad men who were shot by the army when they tried to blow up Gibraltar. We'd been to Gibraltar on holiday and saw the monkeys on the rock. I was glad the army stopped the bad men because they might have hurt the monkeys who did nothing to nobody except steal a packet of cigarettes from Dad's pocket. We all laughed, and he scowled and went after the monkey like he did us when we needed to be punished for something.

Mum gasped at the pictures on the TV. Then there was a

hushed exchange between her and Dad that ended with Dad saying loudly, Slap it up them, and then turning his back to her. There was a note of weary anger behind the thin veneer of satisfaction that I didn't understand. Later, I assumed he was glad because someone was prepared to treat the bad men the way they treat others, like maybe that's the only thing that would stop them. I remember thinking it must be like when the neighbour's dog pooed in our garden, and Dad caught him and sprayed him with the hose. There was still poo in the garden, but my dad was sure the dog learned its lesson. At least until the next day when that damned dog came back again with an arse full of shite.

Dad shouted at the TV, seeing Gerry Adams crouched behind a child, calling him all the cowardly bastards of the day. Dad always got angry when Gerry Adams was on. He remembered him when he was a barman in the 60s. Now he was all over the airwaves, his words spoken by an actor as if that would rob them of their power. It kinda did. He always seemed ridiculous talking like he was in a badly dubbed martial arts movie. I asked if they did that because he had a silly voice, like all high-pitched, and my dad scoffed. No, son, he said, his face turning mournful.

Dad's jaw rocked from side to side when I asked about the farmer man at the funeral.

Is he one of the bad men too?

Why does he want to kill those people?

Did they kill someone he loved?

Are they the men who blew up your shop, Dad? Dad?

He said I ask too many questions.

How many questions are too many? I asked with genuine curiosity, and he answered with a swift kick at me with the side of his foot.

We never had much luck with funerals here. Three days later two soldiers drove the wrong way into the funeral of the people the farmer man killed. We watched it on the news too. It scared the life out of me, seeing people tearing at them like hyenas attacking a gazelle. They pulled those poor young fellas from their car and beat them bloody before shooting them in the head. A priest kneeled beside them and whispered in their ears. I wanted to know if he was telling them how to get to heaven. I was worried he'd give them the wrong directions because Dad said never to trust a priest.

Mum bit her lip and held back tears. Dad thumped the table making me jump. Look at them, didn't I tell ye? he said. They'd see every one of us like that given the chance.

The atmosphere hung in the room for ages, like the smoke billowing from Dad's pursed lips, only dispersing when *Beadle's About* came on. It always made Dad roar his leg off between big gulps of cider and long pulls on another freshly lit cigarette. When I looked at Mum to see if she was laughing too, I'd catch her with that empty look on her face that she'd break, just for me, smiling so hard tears would form in the corner of her eyes.

# The Art of Losing

Samantha Fern

There's a list, a 'Mum-care' list, that you recite to yourself each day. You'll never write it down. Your role reversal would unravel, if Mum were to find it:

> *Water her plants. Keep them alive, keep death away from this house. Fill her fridge. Dilute her wine bottles with tap water. Cook her spaghetti. Hug her in the morning. Hug her before bed. Squeeze tight, hold the back of her head. Compliment her once each day. Laugh when she laughs. Tell her stories about work. Tell her anything that has nothing to do with Dad. Play board games with her. Lose them. Wear headphones when listening to music. It makes her cry. All of it. Pretend to be fine. Make it believable. You have one parent left. Keep her happy. Keep her healthy. Keep her alive.*

You'll stay here in Mum's house, Dad's house, your

childhood home. You'll stay with Mum until the dust settles, although you wonder if it ever will.

You look through Mum's photo albums today, the fourth day since Dad's death. Designer by trade, artist at heart, you need to see him. You need natural shots tastefully framed, a decorative shrine to a man who always dressed flamboyantly. So you photocopy two pictures of him and slide them into pale wooden frames. One from the month before he died, looking gaunt and serious. One a decade old, of the fat, chuckling man you knew, more Santa than Egyptian mummy. *Charming, Whiz*, you hear him say.

You pick up Santa Dad, hold his laughing upper body in your hands. You close your eyes. You bring his face to mind. It's the huge brown irises that come to you. And his skull – a shape you never expected, a nutcracker, all chalk and cheek, all mechanics.

You try and banish his haunting skeleton by summoning the fat man, the man you spent your energy insulting, to bring him down a peg. To make him laugh. You remember being so small your whole body could fit on his belly. He was an ocean to you, as you rose and fell with his tidal breaths.

Opening your eyes, you try to absorb this picture into your subconscious. Telling stories between his wrinkles to help you remember. You realise you've stopped breathing, your fingertips white with the tightness of their grip. A hairline crack splinters across the glass. Across his neck, beheading him.

You've walked to Catford high street for no particular reason, just to leave the house. You wander into Card

Factory, drawn in by the bright colours and joy for sale. But you find yourself staring at the label *BIRTHDAY CARDS FOR DAD*. You can't stop yourself from reading every single one.

> *No. 1 Dad!*
> *Happy Birthday Dad*
> *TO A SUPER DAD*

You press your finger into the word 'Dad' on each card.

> *Five-star parenting, I turned out amazing*
> *DAD, I will always be your ~~little girl~~ financial*
> *burden*

You think about his last birthday, his fifty-fourth. It's mostly a blur of your aunts and uncles topping up your wine glass, but you remember what you got him. Knee-high slipper boots, with dog faces. He laughed at them, but Mum told you weeks later that he wore them every lazy Sunday morning.

> *Dad I've grown up to be just like you! But*
> *slimmer and much better looking . . .*
> *Here's a special card for one of my favourite*
> *parents!*

If you're honest with yourself, he was your favourite. Mum is the bad cop, the tough love, the brutal honesty. Dad was the soft voice of reason, the firm 'Hey!' when Mum got personal, the gentle knock at the door five minutes after you stormed up to your room when you were a teenager.

> *I forgot to put money in this card, but at your age, you've probably forgotten it's your birthday anyway so . . . Merry Christmas Dad!*
> *I can't believe you made it to 60 you fat bastard!*

You glare at that number, 60. You can feel your face twisting into an ugly, unfamiliar shape. You can't stop yourself – you rip the card in two and hide the pieces inside the envelope. You swallow the lump in your throat and blink away the moisture in your eyes, desperate not to cry in the middle of the shop.

> *Happy 70th to an amazing dad and an even better granddad*

You won't have children. What's the point? He will never meet them.

> *Olive you Dad*

He would joke that all he did was drop you. That your children will be safer without his clumsy hands.

At Tesco, you choose food at random, feeling no hunger, having no plan for such useless items as a seeded wholemeal loaf or soba noodles. But you must force Mum to eat. You must lead by example.

You're unpacking now in her kitchen, slowly, like a cloud drifting across the sky. Rolling from one cupboard to the next, to the fridge, to the freezer. You have one item left, at the bottom of a Bag for Life. It's cold, wet, bulky. You pull it out to discover a pack of four Budweisers.

You stop breathing.

You don't remember picking these up.

Your heart beats so ferociously, you're afraid Mum will hear it from the next room.

You run for the back door, fight with the handle before you realise the door's locked, so you twist the key with undue violence. But you're too slow. Mum appears in the kitchen doorway, as if she's drawn to pain these days.

'What's that?'

She's looking at the bottles in your hand. You hold them up to her, ten again, showing her the fancy china mugs you broke when you were trying to reach the biscuit barrel.

She presses a finger to the cool, condensed water on the side of a bottle and pulls it away immediately, as if the glass has burned her. She turns and walks back into the living room, holding the sides of her face.

You wrench the back door open and lob the bottles over the fence like a discus thrower. The lager he will never drink again. The lager you bought him. Forgetting, for a few precious, wonderful seconds, that he no longer exists.

The doorbell rings. Dad's in a Ferrari, the top down. This is the kind of dream where you don't have the sense to wonder how he rang the doorbell from three metres away. Or how he bought a car that costs more than the house.

You jump into the front seat like you're in *Ferris*

*Bueller's Day Off.* Dad whizzes you around the neighbourhood, somehow driving through fields you've never noticed before, towards the sunset, along a beach and into the sea. You hold out a hand and skim the waves with your fingers, sea spray in your hair.

You glance at him once, twice. He looks pained.

'Shall I drop you off here?' he asks.

'No no, keep driving.'

'Are you sure I can't drop you off here?' he almost begs. His hands start to shrink, to wither and blacken on the wheel, his whole body shaking.

'What's wrong?'

'Are you sure you can't get out here?'

You panic and jump out of the car into the sea. Treading water, you watch the car vanish over the horizon.

You wake up crying. You feel as if you haven't slept a wink.

Today, you write down a list of compliments about Mum. You must appreciate her while she's here:

> *Her grasp of mathematics fills me with awe.*
> *The way she moves and walks is so graceful,*
> *as if she's always dancing.*
> *Her practicality amazes me. She can fix*
> *things without YouTube.*
> *She has a nice singing voice. It reminds me of*
> *early springtime. I miss hearing it.*
> *She remembers every detail of my childhood,*
> *including what vaccinations I've had, what*
> *hour I was born, what my first, second and*

*third words were ('no', 'dog' and 'ma').*
*When she curls up on the chair in a blanket,*
*she looks like a ripple of water.*
*Sometimes if I wake in the night, I can hear*
*her crying. It's a sound like violins and*
*opera. It feels like a flower opening in my*
*chest. I cannot resist joining in.*

You're seven.

You're the best in your class at skipping. Everyone says so, even Billie who wishes it was her. You skipped one hundred skips in your garden every day for a week to prepare for this. You won the qualifiers (you don't even know the word 'qualifiers', but you won them).

You're at the chalk white line, the red track hazy in the hot sun. Skipping-rope handles turning to eels in your sweaty hands. Here wakes the fluttering robin in your chest, the one that made a nest before you can remember, the one that will lay eggs and multiply into a flock of fluttering birds.

The whistle goes – the moment you've waited for is finally here. And as you fly forwards, the rope a grey smudge of plastic, you realise you're tripping. That your foot has caught in the rope on the very first skip, and you're falling towards the bright-red ground.

You think about the dream you had weeks before, where a gum-coloured leech clung to the back of your knee, like a small, smooth tongue. You woke up trying to bat it away, shivering.

Now you're crying, in front of the mums and dads, in front of your friends. You can't see your parents; all you can see is the blur of your competitors racing into the distance. They seem two streets away, a bus ride away, a whole journey to school away. You fumble forwards before giving up.

You walk straight off the track and into your pen, where all the kids in your House sit on the grass, indifferent to your despair. You join them, tearing blades from the ground, crying. You want to go home.

But then Dad appears, a monument against the sun. He lies on the grass beside you and asks simply, 'You all right?' As if your tiny little world hadn't just ended.

'It doesn't matter, Whiz. Winning is something you carry inside you. Not something you have to do.'

You don't entirely understand, but your mind feels blown anyway. In years to come, you'll wonder if he gave you the secret of life, as you grapple with the edges of it.


You're well used to vivid daydreams. You'll walk to the shop and en route, you'll dance in the middle of a bar on a tabletop to Britney Spears' *Work Bitch*, or you'll save your closest friends from a gang of muggers and rapists and reveal your secret powers and martial arts skills. Sometimes, these moments are barely distinguishable from reality – until you cross the road without looking and get yelled at by an Uber driver.

But this morning, your dad's sitting on your bed. Dad, who's been dead for seven days. He's gaunt, as he was when he died. Wearing his ancient, disintegrating dressing gown. You can feel the mattress dip under his weight. You can sense something in the air, as if it's charged with static electricity. You're telling yourself this is another daydream, but not one cell of your body believes you. The robins in your chest are a storm of wings against your ribs.

'Dad?'

He rises from the bed and starts to walk towards you in a way you don't understand. As if he's an imposter made of kitchenware. The robins have frozen into stone, a crushing weight in your chest.

He's moving faster but also staying in the same spot and you think this must be your life now. Watching Dad claw his way towards you, without ever getting anywhere.

Your phone beeps at you aggressively and you jump a foot into the air. You grab it, swiping 'Off' on your alarm. You look up and Dad's gone. The quilt smooth where he sat.

It's been a day since Dad appeared. You're on the sofa, ignoring *Love Island* – Mum's guilty pleasure. You pick up your phone and search 'are ghosts friendly'. You find a blog that feels like procrastination, so you read the whole thing.

> ### *5 friendly Hollywood ghosts you want to be haunted by*
> 5. *Malcolm Crowe,* The Sixth Sense
> *SPOILER ALERT: STOP READING IF YOU HAVEN'T SEEN* THE SIXTH SENSE. *For starters, who doesn't want Bruce Willis in their home? And bless him, this lost soul doesn't even know he's dead, so in that sense, he's just like you or me, trying to live his life (err, or his death . . . ). Befriending the only person that can see him, a schoolkid, is*

*hella wholesome in our opinion. They end up helping each other out (n'aww) and we'd say that's spooktacularly friendly by paranormal standards!*

*4. Moaning Myrtle, Harry Potter franchise*
*This famous adolescent ghost is a real scream! She can't get friendly enough – if you're a good-looking boy in her bathroom. As well as flirting hard with Harry, she helps him find the Chamber of Secrets, and reveals the clue to the second task in the Triwizard Tournament. Give us More-tle, this ghost's an (un)living legend!*

*3. Nearly Headless Nick, Harry Potter franchise*
*This Harry Potter character (last one, we swear) can chat for hours – no, days. He has an eternity to while away, and he doesn't want to be bored to death (oh, wait . . . ). What better housemate than one always ready for a (figurative) heart-to-heart – just prepare for it to last forever (and ever and ever) . . .*

*2. Ghost of Christmas Present,* The Muppet Christmas Carol
*No one can deny that this ghost is a ray of sunshine we'd all love in our lives, despite the bad tidings he brings. Like a ginger Father Christmas, this muppet is as jovial as a ghost can get. Santa's claws are in, honey, this softie is all felt and fuzz.*

*1. Casper, obviously*
*This spooky cutie wouldn't say boo to a goose! He has a helpful spirit (ahem, he IS a helpful spirit, we should say . . . ) – as long as you're one of the good guys. Plus his own theme song says it all, number one was a no-brainer! Now play us out, Universal Pictures (Casper the frieeeendly ghost).*

It's calmed you to read about friendly ghosts that are both familiar and nostalgic. You go back to Ecosia search and try a different tack. You type 'friendly ghost haunting me'. You tap on a link to a paranormal forum, Ghost Spotters.

<u>*I think I'm being haunted by a sweety ghost*</u>
**LeoRising555**
*I think I'm being haunted by a sweety ghost, please help me!*
*It keeps helpfully finding me things I've lost or hiding my chocolate bars to help me deal with a new diagnosus (of diabetus). I think it might be my ex who died in a car crash 5 yrs ago.*
*How do I help it move on? And if its not my ex, how do I find out? And how can I know it won't turn against me?*
**Posted 2 years 5 months ago | Active 3 months ago | Viewed 1.2m times**
   *– C11MOONESS*
   *You're lucky it's a friendly ghost, for now*

*. . . ! Be careful, it might not remain so if it becomes frustrated. Burn sage around your home to get rid of bad energy and unwanted spirits.*
*– MADMAIDEN42*

*I had to move house. Had a ghost that moved things around, like all the stuff on my coffee table would get rearranged. It eventually pulled my shelving unit down and I knew I had to leave.*
*– BADDADDY9!*

*Tell your ex how you feel about them in your house, what they can do to help you (ie leave!)*
*– REALTALK991*

*Just stop watching Netflix horrors amiright?*

You go back to the search bar and start typing 'scientific evidence ghosts exist'. But you stop on 'g'. You'd always thought people who believed in ghosts were burying their heads in the sand. That they'd lost someone too vital and had traded in reality for a bit of hope. You finally understand. If letting go of reality means seeing your dad again, the trade seems perfectly fair.

You're here again, in the very worst moment of your life.

You wake up at 2:26 a.m. because of a noise downstairs. A rattling sound. Like a handful of biros hitting a bare floor.

You rush down the stairs and into the utility room, where Dad's hospital bed is. He's half hanging out of it, trying to get up. A tangle of snappable limbs and plastic tubes. Punctured skin and wasting muscle. You think of bagpipes.

'Dad stop, what's wrong?'

'No,' he breathes.

'I don't want to,' he mouths.

You think he refers to getting back into bed. In the days ahead, when you relive and relive and relive this moment, you'll realise this is not the case.

You tuck him into his sheets. You give him a squeeze, a kiss on the cheek, sit with him for an hour. He wheezes. He wheezes. Then you go back to bed, exhausted.

You wake up as if electrocuted at 5:09 a.m. You hear wailing. You run downstairs. You sprint to the utility room, but the door is sticky, and as you force it open you knock a mug off the desk and onto the floor. It smashes instantly. Your mum doesn't notice.

'HE'S DEAD,' she screams at you.


You're fifteen.

You're top of the class again for another exam that doesn't count for anything. You're telling Dad but you're not sure why. You know your parents are less proud, more worried. That you're not cool, that you're weird, that you're lonely. Maybe you want them to worry.

'Again? Blimey, Liz. Brainbox.'

It reassures you to hear people call you things like this. Smart arse. Neek. It's how you define yourself, this intelligence. You cling tightly to this positive way to frame who you are.

He surprises you by saying, 'You can't always be the best, you know.'

You shrug, pink with that angsty pride and embarrassment that always come hand in hand for you.

'I promise, there'll be something you're not good at one day. You can't keep this up forever.'

You decide that you can, but you nod as if suddenly wiser with his imparted knowledge.

You find out years later, in lectures you cannot follow, on Tinder dates you cut mercifully short, in wine bottles that leave you as empty as you leave them, that he was right. That you cannot keep this up. That you are losing, as promised. That you have lost. That you never learned the art.

Your brother, Adam, pops round in the evenings for dinner, but he never stays long. The house makes him feel uneasy, you can see it in the way he stares at the food on his plate and never makes it past the kitchen. He messages you each morning, from a distance.

> *Found this pic today*
> *Forgot how huge he was, before*
>
> > *Haaa*
> > *That was his 50th!*
>
> *Yeah*
> *We all got trashed*
>
> > *Nah*
> > *Just Aunt Bobby*
> > *She broke 4 glasses*
>
> *Lol*

You resent him for staying at his. For not joining this

grief capsule to suffer with you. He probably plays zombie games on his PS4. While you're pausing at every photo of Dad hung on the wall or propped up on a side table.

You're carrying two tote bags, containing a couple of cartons of apple juice and enough food to fill Mum's fridge. They're so heavy you can barely move yourself forwards. The sky is entirely white, as if you're not outside but are in fact in an igloo. Your breath mists the air and your ears and nose are red with cold.

Since you passed the post box, you've been lambasting yourself for forgetting dental floss (which you thought of because like all designers, you picture parcels tied with string).

You start to think about being homeless, how cold it must be. Your whole body feels as if it has fallen into your shoes and dripped out through the hole in the sole, to suction to the pavement – like stringy cheese in a pizza box.

You realise you're slowing down, grinding to a halt. You look up at the white pressing in on you all around.

You consider sitting down on the ground as the bags start to slide to the tips of your fingers. You even bend your knees, ready to stoop down.

And before you can stop yourself, you're on the corpse-cold pavement, surrounded by bags, a stray potato rolling in front of you across a ground-in blob of gum. You place your hands very calmly on your knees, tracing small circles around the caps with your fingers. You rock ever so slightly and look up. You feel a great bond with the sky. You feel the same vapid density. Nothing to hold onto. Everything to carry.

A Great Dane has curled into a sleeping ball on your chest, merging with the huge military coat your mum got you the Christmas before last. You feel your eyes closing. You want to lie down and sleep for a hundred years. You want snow to fall, you want to be buried in it.

'Are you all right?' a concerned elderly man asks, stopping next to you and leaning heavily on his walking stick. Mocking you with his wrinkled skin, his flat cap, his long life. You can almost hear teenage voices calling him 'Granddad'.

'Oh, I just feel a bit dizzy. I'll get up in a minute.'

'Shall I call someone for you? Or an ambulance?'

'No, no, I'm fine.'

You see that he's going to wait around until you get up. So you sigh, tired by this insistence of 'carrying on'. Embarrassed somewhere deep down in your body.

You find momentum from somewhere, the cookie-dough reindeer you just ate perhaps, and you get up. You carry on.


Dad's been dead for eleven days and now here you are, in a black pencil skirt and kitten heels you call your 'funeral shoes'. Mum says you're too young to have footwear dedicated to death.

You feel excruciatingly sexy in this outfit. This is also half your job-interview ensemble. The skirt is past your knees but clings to your figure. It gives you boss-bitch, power-suit vibes, something that helps you strut into meeting rooms and blag your way into new jobs. Today, it makes you walk like Bambi as you try to keep your butt tucked in, to quash your curves and confidence under the black gravity of grief. You'll soon have some money to buy more clothes, courtesy of Dad's life insurance. So you don't have to feel attractive when you're burying your family members. But you know you won't spend the money on dedicated wakewear.

You're cold – your skin-coloured tights laddered as you pulled them on and, even though Dad wouldn't give a flying fuck, it felt disrespectful wearing ripped tights to his funeral. So you're bare-legged, knees knocking together (Mum told you to borrow her stockings, but then the hearse was outside, and it didn't seem to matter anymore).

You ignore the priest blathering on about a stranger, confusing you and your brother ('his eldest, Elizabeth'). You stare at the coffin, closed, sealed. Your uncle, Pete, flattens a piece of paper at the lectern, clears his throat.

'My first memory of my brother is from when I was about four. He wouldn't let me ride his bike, he said it was too dangerous.' He takes a moment, looks up into the rafters. 'Even when I stabbed you in the ankle with a pen, you didn't let me ride it, you little shit.'

The crowd titters, although Mum stiffens next to you. You look over and see a struggle on her face that you've seen before. She's trying not to cry. You lean into her arm, offering the only comfort that won't make her feel inadequate.

'I remember, when the biro went in, there was so much blood. I panicked. I hadn't really meant to do it. I went white as a sheet and nearly fainted. And what did Rob do?' He pauses to take a shaky breath. 'He got me a glass of water. Sat me down. Gave me a cookie. With a pen sticking out of his ankle.' He chokes, 'ankle' becoming 'an-khanahalah' as tears and snot melt his face into something you want to turn away from.

'That's the man he was – even when he was eight. He was too good for us. Even then.'

He tears his paper from the lectern and snivels as he returns to his seat.

You'd never heard that story before. You hold those last words in your fingers, which you've clasped together in your lap. They sweat and sweat but you cannot unclasp them. Because they're glued together. *He was too good for us.*

At the wake, people are shaking your clammy hands, people you feel guilty for not recognising. You bung a cucumber sandwich into your mouth and take what feels like half an hour to chew it down.

You walk round and round the perimeter of the pub your mum booked, trying to lose the crowd. If you stay in one place for any length of time, an old colleague of Dad's or a slurring aunt twice removed will find you and scramble for ways to make you feel better. Pulling clichés out of the air, nodding their heads gently.

It's a bizarre charade to you right now. This isn't some wedding or birthday party. You can't wrap your head around why people have dressed up and drunk wine to 'celebrate' your one precious father being wiped from this earth. From your life. Forever.

You walk past a middle-aged woman in a black-and-white flowery dress stumbling towards the roses in the pub garden, crouching down to vomit into their unravelling faces. A man who you assume is her husband, silver whiskers frothed with Guinness, hurries to her, holds back her hair.

You think about what Dad would have said. You know he'd have brought her a glass of water, without saying a thing – so as not to embarrass her. She would have drunk it, oblivious, thanking her husband for somehow fetching this miraculous liquid whilst also holding her hair.

*He was too good for us.*

It's been eighteen days since he died and the bouquets upon bouquets of flowers now slowly rot in Mum's garden-waste bin.

You eat three meals a day.

You've stopped mentioning him.

You set three places at the table each night, for you, Mum and Adam.

You plaster on a smile.

You laugh.

You want to go home but you're terrified of leaving Mum alone in this house. Terrified of leaving Dad, in this house. His wardrobe still bulging with clothes. Dustings of his skin still contained in the sleeves. On the carpets. In the crevices of his armchair.

Mum sits in the latter every night. The cushions still flattened in an imprint of him – you can almost see his brightly clad belly heaving up and down with each breath. It's the only place you still see him as a fat man; years of watching *Star Trek* together have been tattooed into your brain. You want to tell Mum to get up, to get away. She will change the imprint. He will be gone.

You catch snatches of grief on your own where you can. You don't do it around your family, not when Adam pops round each night, not when Mum pours ever larger glasses of wine with lunch and dinner.

You visit graveyards and hang around churches, on your lunch breaks, on your weekends. You watch the bereaved closely, grasping for any clues on surviving the ravages of grief. There's a graveyard near your office and you've lingered by two weeping mourners so far. You closed your eyes and breathed in their shuddering despair, finding comfort in it. You felt the pull of the abyss, recognised the way they leaned towards it, peering into a darkness few others could see. Here it is, you thought. Here is the world coming to an end.

Today is Sunday and you've managed to find a funeral. You lurked by your local church, dressed in black, all day Saturday but to no avail. You came back early this morning and now, two hours later, a hearse is pulling up.

White chrysanthemums spell *Nan* and *Mum*. The coffin is a dark stained wood. A thick oak. She'll be safe in there, you think.

You stand at the back of the church and watch a family carry the coffin down the aisle on their shoulders. You cry throughout the service. You weep and weep.

'She was always losing her glasses. And they were always tied around her neck.'

'She always sent coupons in the mail for her grandchildren.'

'She loved teasing us – we believed her middle name was "Elspeth" for fifteen years.'

Your focus isn't on the eulogies or the priest at the front of the church. You're scanning the mourners. You watch a young man in the front row bawl over the word 'piano'.

You inhale the yell of a small child, 'Nana!' You choke on the sight of a father holding his daughter as she sobs into his shoulder.

You flee the scene just before the end of the service, as *You Raise Me Up* begins to play and a great howling erupts that you cannot identify as male, female, young or old.

You get home in time to find Mum in front of one of her beloved quiz shows. You fall onto the sofa and she tells the TV it's Mexico, obviously Mexico. She laughs at Lee Mack. You always make sure to get home in time for this. In time to hear your mum laughing at Lee Mack.

# A Day at the Beach

Sophia Khan

In the unlikely spirit of an unhappy family, Ammu suddenly announced that we were going to the beach for the day.

It was the summer of 1987 and the thermometer had hit thirty-three degrees. The flat was sticky, overwhelmed by the heat from the laundrette downstairs. Boredom flourished. Pinky and I had argued so much over what to watch on TV that we were no longer talking. 'We're going,' Ammu said as she came out of the bathroom and into the living room. She was wearing a light-blue cotton maxi dress, ritually dotting Astral cream onto her forehead, cheeks and chin before smearing it into her face until it shone like a coffee bean.

'Pinky, Rekha, cholo.'

'Going where?' Pinky asked but Ammu had disappeared into the kitchen. A wave of grease from the food fryer unravelled as we packed jalebis, samosas and onion bhajis into empty ice cream containers. Baba was nowhere in sight until we were sealed in the car, boiling hot from lugging the food down two flights of stairs. He sauntered down, car keys jangling in his hand. Pinky, who had applied thick black eyeliner and blue mascara, was scowling under her heavy fringe. Patches of sweat formed on the back of my dress. Ammu had insisted on using new hair bobbles from Woolworths, tightly plaiting my hair until my scalp hurt.

Baba started puffing away on cigarette after cigarette once we were on the A40. 'We came to Brighton a very long time ago, soon after your ammu and I got married.' He sounded grizzly, but eager to start a conversation. No one said anything. Ammu started to check the contents of bags that sat between her legs. He carried on, oblivious to the silence. 'It was just after we had arrived in London and everyone was dressing like Mick Jagger and women had their hair cut like this.' He made a blunt action with his hand across his face. Pinky got out a biro from her back pocket. 'That's called a bob,' she said as she started doodling on her thumb. 'Ha, yes, bob,' Baba said as if remembering a fact he had forgotten.

The car smelt of cigarettes and curry. Stony buildings faded as we left the city.

Ammu put her palm to her forehead as we approached the motorway.

'Oh Allah, we need to go back.'

'Ki?' Baba asked, confused, before switching lanes. A shiny gleam of sweat was forming on his brow.

'We have to go back. I forgot my purse,' she said in Bangla.

'It's fine,' Baba said. 'No problem, I have my wallet.'

'I had some money to give to the children.'

'I have money too,' he said brusquely.

'No, you don't understand,' Ammu said with panic rising in her voice. 'I have it. I wanted to give it to them.'

Baba's neck stiffened as he clenched his jaws. The

back of his head was glossy with oil. 'We can't go back, we're too far.'

'But I had the money.'

'Well you should have remembered instead of crying down the phone to your fucking sister.'

Pinky stopped doodling. I opened my purse and fiddled around with my lip balm. We had both heard crying the night before but neither of us had left our beds. Baba had been out all night.

He wound his window down and lit another cigarette. Pinky took the cassette out of her Walkman, 'summer '87 Prince & co' scrawled across in blue biro. She used her small finger to wind the tape back, inserted it with a click, and pressed Play.

Ammu sat still. Every now and then her right hand rose, wiping at her face gently. Baba puffed away, his fingers tapping against the steering wheel.

I looked out of the window as we sped along the endless stretch of motorway. There were fields of green with patches of yellow where the grass had been scorched. Sheep and horses stood grazing, flanked by towering pylons, alarming against the blue sky. Cars and trucks thundered along. Ammu and Pinky didn't say a word. Occasionally Baba hummed a tune. There were more roads after coming off the motorway, then a confusion of roundabouts followed by rows of houses which seemed charmed by being near the sea. Seeing them stirred a hope in me that the day could still turn out well. We came to the town centre where a neat line of blue glimmered beyond the shops. The sight of the ocean made Ammu sit up and instantly start rummaging in her bag for her disposable camera.

It was almost midday and unbearably hot. I was wearing Pinky's old sandals and could feel the scorch of the pavement. Baba straightened out his polo top and shorts. He took a small plastic comb from his back pocket and combed his hair to one side whilst looking in the window. His toes wriggled around in his Batas. The hairs on his arms and legs were thick and long. He took out a small green pot of chun paste and rubbed it onto the paan leaf before chewing it ferociously.

'Out the way, Fat Face,' Pinky said, elbowing me as she helped Ammu unload the car.

We all waddled along the beach, weighed down by the ice boxes, blankets, beach towels and flasks of tea and coffee. The beach was full and crowded. Ammu started winding the gear on the camera before handing it to Pinky who was busy finding a free spot for us to sit.

'There, there!' It was Ammu who had finally found one, pointing at an empty patch that only she could see. Her footsteps quickened and we walked hurriedly to keep up with her. 'Uff,' Baba said in frustration as small stones slid into his sandals. A couple who had also been vying for the spot looked at all of us. The young man glanced at Baba and then whispered in his girlfriend's ear causing her to laugh. I unfolded the blanket with Ammu, a bewildering sense of hurt stirring within me.

Ammu was now in charge, directing me and my sister. A huge umbrella with an Abbey National logo fanned open to shade us from the sun. 'Pinky, put the ice box *here*. Rekha, lay the blanket with me, hold the corners.' Baba was busy pouring himself a coffee. My stomach lurched around in hunger as I eyed up the crisps, samosas and mini rolls. Ammu gave me a carton of juice. 'Rekha, the straw, pierce it properly.'

'It's going to spill. She's not listening,' Pinky said as I kept jabbing the carton with my chubby fingers.

A huge liquid bruise on my dress as blackcurrant juice spilt.

'Told you,' Pinky said.

Baba laughed and shook his head.

I burst into tears.

'Come on,' Pinky said, taking off her Converse trainers and socks, leaving the camera with Ammu.

'Not too high, Pinky,' Baba said, watching her closely as she rolled up her jeans.

She glared at him and then stretched her hand towards me. 'C'mon, we'll wash it out in the sea and I'll teach you how to skim stones.'

The blood-warm water cooled our blisteringly hot feet. Pinky rolled up her jeans even further so they sat at the very top of her thighs, exposing the purple lines of her knickers. She bent into the water and peered carefully. A group of children were shouting to each other as they frantically swam after a beach ball.

'The trick is to look for a smooth one. One that's very flat,' Pinky said, meticulously examining the stones through her sunglasses. She inspected each of them one by one before tossing them back into the sea.

I scooped water into my hands, enjoying the feeling of my dress getting drenched. I showed Pinky the cliffs, chalky and white, only for her to point out that they were buildings, possibly hotels.

'OK now watch,' she said. She had slid her sunglasses

onto the top of her head and her Michael Jackson T-shirt was tied in a huge knot above her belly button. A slit at the top had been made to expose the fold between her growing breasts. She outstretched her left arm for balance and with the other, threw the pebble fast and low. I watched as it skipped across the water, bouncing several times before disappearing. Every time it was my turn, I failed again and again.

'You'll learn,' she said before splashing me.

As we walked back, I could make out where Baba and Ammu sat. Unlike the other couples, they were sitting apart. Ammu had her legs straight out in front of her, her hair blowing freely. From the distance, she looked like a mixture of Diana Ross and Madhuri Dixit.

'Do you think Ammu is less sad now?' I asked Pinky.

'What do you mean?' She was fishing around in her pocket for her lip balm. The pen-drawn tattoo had mostly washed off her hand.

'He made her sad in the car.'

Pinky sighed. 'He always makes her sad.'

'Why?'

She slowly shrugged in a way that revealed she didn't fully understand either.

'Does Baba love us?'

'In his own way. Yes.' She said this doubtfully.

'So that means he doesn't really then, does he?'

She looked at me curiously. A cloud came over her face, casting a shadow that veiled her eyes. 'It means whatever you want it to mean,' she said, and distracted me by making us race back to the blankets. Ammu smiled at us as we got closer. She had applied her favourite lipstick and looked almost radiant. Baba stood up to survey the scene around him, hand on waist, loftier but out of place.

Ammu started assigning us roles again.

'Pinky, open that box. Rekha, you give out the plates and forks.'

The food was laid out in all its glory, luring seagulls that we tried to shoo away. Pinky started nibbling on a corner of samosa. 'Only one samosa?' Ammu asked. Pinky shrugged. Baba took copious amounts of everything and ate furiously, with bits of moori sticking to the side of his mouth before dropping off. He kept chewing and eating and talking as he continued to help himself. Every time he spoke, I could see the contents of his mouth. Sometimes drops of water would land on his chin as he gulped it down.

I heaped my plate with hot food, topping it with salt and vinegar crisps and a slice of halwa. Ammu tried to attack her kichori with a fork before giving up and using her fingers.

'The sea reminds me of Bangladesh,' she said, after swallowing her food. Her words came out of her like a murmur, half dream-like and almost wistful.

'Ha,' Baba said, nodding in agreement.

'Which way takes you to Dhaka?' Pinky asked. Her palms were flat, either side of her, and she was sitting with her legs out. The soles of her feet were covered in sand and stones.

'Ahh well, let's see now, maybe north-west,' Baba said, pointing in a certain direction. 'You know, people think of Bangladesh as just this poor country that gets flooded but it is so much more than that.' His plate was finally empty and he laid it to one side. 'We actually come from such strong stock, you know? Our bloody history, our ancestry and Bengali culture overall. It's so much more than Tagore and *Pather Panchali.*'

For the first time that day he looked at me, playfully reaching out to flick the hair bobbles on my plaits. Pinky had slipped on her headphones. Ammu was looking out at the sea, deep in thought. Her soft belly poked through the hole in her maxi dress. Her legs were swollen from constant standing at the factory where she worked. She had pulled me towards her and untied my hair, freshly plaiting it with the hair bobbles in her mouth. Baba, who had abruptly stopped talking, stood up with a piece of paper in his hand.

'Tumi kothay jaccho? Where are you going?' Ammu asked.

'I need to make a phone call.'

'To who?'

'Sultan, you know Sultan. He is having problems with his visa.'

'I thought you said Sultan had gone back to desh.'

'No, no, he still needs my help.'

'And you need to call him now?'

'Ha,' Baba said. 'Yes.'

He smoothed his hair to one side and took out a cigarette. His gold chain glinted in the sunlight. Ammu moved me aside and fell silently within herself, clutching a pink comb she had removed from her bag. She slowly started combing her hair. Her mouth was moving but no words were audible.

'How long will you be?' Pinky asked. 'Because we want to go to the pier and you didn't drive back for Ammu's purse.'

'I'm not sure,' Baba said, his eyes narrowing.

'Can't you leave *her* alone for just one day?' Ammu said all of a sudden.

'Leave who alone?' I said, puzzled. No one heard me. Baba ignored Ammu. Pinky interjected.

'OK, we'll wait then,' she said, her voice measured but straining to keep things normal.

Ammu rose as Baba walked away.

'Watch my bag,' she said to us. Her murmuring voice had been torn away to reveal fresh, hard anger.

'Ammu, where are you going? Can I come?' I could hear the panic in my own voice. But she had started drifting off towards the sea. Walking as if she was drunkenly dazed by the heat.

We watched as Ammu entered the water, wading further and further into it until her maxi dress was fully soaked and her hair fanned out on the surface of the water. She took off her maxi dress and tossed it across the waves, her greying bra and knickers stretched taut across her yielding body.

Pinky was standing up, peering with intense concentration, her eyes following Ammu's movements.

'What is she doing?'

'Come on,' Pinky said, grabbing Ammu's bag and my arm. We ran towards the sea leaving everything abandoned. She dumped Ammu's bag on the sand and we both plunged in. Ammu saw us, and a wild, free smile came over her face. In a frenzy she was splashing us and we were splashing her, laughing hysterically, recklessly, roaring with uncontrollable glee. Pinky seized Ammu's maxi dress and lovingly slipped it back on her.

We walked back to the blankets, dizzy with the heat.

That cool aching wind, like passages of time, caressed our backs and arms. Baba had returned and was sitting on the blanket, chomping on a samosa, a small bottle of whisky by his foot. His eyes were drunk and furious.

'What the fuck is this?'

'Ki?' Ammu replied.

'Your clothes . . . It's horrible.' I had never seen him look at Ammu with such clear disgust. 'You look so ugly.'

'Don't talk to her like that,' Pinky said.

'Don't you young girls tell me how to talk! You Western girls! No respect for your parents.'

Finally it dawned on me that nobody actually wanted to be there, none of us, not even me. Other people nearby were looking in our direction.

'I wanted to enjoy the sea.'

'By taking your clothes off so all these men could look at you? Where is your respect? Your faith? We are Muslim. God, look at you. You're a mess. Filthy.'

Pinky butted in. 'Well you're drunk and you sneak off to talk to your . . . friends, so who's being a good Muslim now?'

Baba clenched his fists. He probably would have slapped Pinky across the face had it not been for where we were. Instead he scowled at Ammu. 'You can't do anything right. You can't even bring your girls up right. See how they disrespect me?'

I ran to Ammu and cocooned my face in her stomach. Her dress felt wet and coarse against my skin but the ends of her hair were warming in the sun as they dried. Baba carried on drinking. We started tidying the things away.

'Why don't you ever talk back to him and stand up for

yourself?' Pinky whispered fiercely in Ammu's ear as she helped to pack up.

Ammu ignored her. Pinky threw a handful of cutlery down on the ground.

'Fuck this,' she said and stomped off.

'Stop her,' Ammu said to Baba.

'I won't,' Baba said. 'She'll be at the car.'

By the time we had packed everything away and lugged all the nearly empty containers to the car, Baba was beginning to sober up and confusingly, Ammu was nodding her head as he spoke about how being by the sea made him want to catch fish like he used to as a child in Bangladesh. 'You know, none of this cod bullshit. Proper fish like ilish and rui.'

Pinky was leaning against the bonnet with her arms folded, studying them both closely.

Our mother was determined that Pinky and I would get what she promised us. 'We are going to take the children to the pier and the arcade,' she said to Baba, who nodded. He was sullen, he looked beaten down and his hair was no longer smooth. I hesitantly went towards him and held his hand.

We headed towards the pier. Two men were kissing on a park bench.

'Tauba, tauba, revolting,' Baba said.

'You're revolting,' Pinky muttered behind him.

But he seemed puffed up. 'We should visit the Pavilion one day. See how the British were inspired by Indian architecture. How they took what India had to offer and stole it for their own greed and good. Just because we are in Englishmen's country doesn't mean we should forget.'

The smell of fish and chips and deep-fried doughnuts led us to the pier where we could hear Whitney Houston blaring out of a radio. There was a throng of sunburnt skin, flip-flops, the sounds of buckets and spades rattling in the slow breeze, dogs barking, skinheads shouting, punks smoking, the bright colours of the fairground rides in the distance, the glimpse of blue sea through the wooden slats. We could hear the pinball machines and the buzz from the arcade. An older man winked at Pinky which she pretended to ignore. She was intrigued by everything she had seen. Holding my hand firmly, she showed me all of the different games.

'Give them five pounds each,' Ammu said to Baba.

'No way,' Baba said. 'Too much. They can share five pounds between them. Or Pinky can have three pounds because she is older.'

'No,' Ammu replied firmly. Her hair had been tied into a loose bun, making her features look sharper. 'I had five pounds saved up for them each. It's what I want for them.'

Baba reluctantly reached into his back pocket then rubbed his chin before opening his wallet. Inside, there were a few notes. He gave us each five pounds. We walked in and went to the counter to change our money before going to the slot machines. Pinky had her plastic tub of coins and I held mine. Slowly, I took out as many 2p coins as would fit within the palm of my hand. Baba said he was going outside for a cigarette.

We played all the games but came back to the grab machine because Ammu wanted a heart-shaped key ring. She perched herself on the edge of a stool watching Pinky and me shriek in delight when we won it for her. Pinky told

Ammu that she needed the toilet.

'I want to come,' I said.

I followed her and waited outside. She rolled her eyes when I told her I didn't really need to go, I just wanted to be with her. I wandered around the corner of the arcade, past the grab machines and the slot machines. There were two young men who looked so alike and dressed so alike, I couldn't tell if they were brothers or lovers. In the distance I spotted Baba. He was leaning against one of the machines. His mouth was moving around and there was a softness around his lips and something arresting in his eyes. He was talking to a woman wearing a sarong and a white bikini top. Her brown hair looked like it was starting to turn blond in the sun. She had her hand on his arm and was whispering something into his ear. His fingers were almost stroking her stomach. They looked like they were about to lean in and kiss each other.

'Are you sure you don't need the toilet?' Pinky was behind me, hand on her hip.

I shook my head. Out of loyalty to Baba, I distracted Pinky away from what I had seen. I dragged her to the machines on the other side of the arcade. Whatever I had seen, my eight-year-old self understood what it meant to carry a secret. A sullen kind of pride washed over me for fooling her. On our way, we passed Ammu laughing to herself at the grab machine. 'Look at what I won for us,' she said, holding two small teddies and a kaleidoscope. 'Rekha, you have the kaleidoscope.' I took the bright-green tube but something had twisted within me. It felt dense, heavy and unflinching.

Baba appeared after a few minutes. He seemed flushed

and was smoothing down his hair. He wouldn't look at any of us directly.

'This was fun,' Ammu said. 'Rekha, say thank you to your baba for the money he gave you.'

I didn't.

'Chi, Rekha.'

Baba stared at me affectionately and came to embrace me but I stepped out of the way. A look of surprise came over him. He looked guilty and hurt.

We left the pier and walked back to the car, our shadows no longer short and squat but tall and thin. Baba started the engine and got out one of his cassettes, forcing us to listen to songs from the *Mr India* movie.

Once we got home, Ammu gave Pinky some money to develop the photos, which she collected on her way home from school a few days later. When Pinky showed them to me, all of them apart from one were of us three in the sea, taken from a distance. The last one was of the sea alone. There were none of Ammu or Baba together.

Years later, when she had just moved to California with her girlfriend, Pinky and I were on the phone. She said that she was walking on the beach and saw a woman with a long maxi dress and thick, wavy hair. Far away it was the spitting image of Ammu.

But both of us knew it wasn't.

# Entanglement

David Micklem

The sun is low over their pool, and it really is a gorgeous evening, warm and still, when I spot him silhouetted over Tim's shoulder. I catch his outline for a second and even though he's just a shape and he lives a thousand miles away, I know it's him.

My arm is draped through Simon's but I withdraw it as soon as I think I see him, without thinking. Simon is saying something to Tim about a vacation we took to Greece and he turns and looks at me and my arm and continues talking.

'It's where Homer sets *The Odyssey*.'

I concentrate hard to make my face appear normal again. I'm sure it will have contorted into something pained and frightened but neither Simon, nor Tim, nor Tim's wife who is smoking flamboyantly, seem to have noticed.

My sunglasses are on my head, largely to keep my hair off my face, and I put them on and look out across the pool to the edge of the Baxters' land. A row of ironwoods mark the boundary between their manicured and tended property and open desert to the south and west and the Ortiz Mountains beyond. To the side is a large paddock marked by a barbed-wire fence. A pair of horses nibble at hay in a feeder. One paws at the ground and the sun catches the dust it kicks up.

I fake an interest in a mountain laurel at the far side of the pool but behind my huge frames my eyes are darting between the guests, desperate to prove my earlier sighting wrong.

There are perhaps forty people gathered out on the raised concrete deck that runs from inside the house right to the lip of the pool. Small groups served by a hired waitress who shuttles back and forth with a tray of drinks. Simon and I know Tim and his wife from the gallery which we all support. I know Tracey Mulrose who I saw when we arrived and who's standing in the shade with Lydia Baxter. Lydia is always at the tennis club and her husband Ted is something big in tech and I'm amazed he's even here.

I scan the party, lit golden by the last of the sun before it winks below the blue wall of the mountain range. A line of bare bulbs that are draped between olive trees in a zigzag across the deck flick on.

Lydia is wearing a dress I nearly bought but decided made me look older than I am.

I drain my gin and tonic and wave at the girl in the black pants and crisp white shirt who's already spotted me. I've had three and for a moment I convince myself I was just a little lightheaded, that I was seeing things.

I can picture him standing over me, his teeth gritted, sweat beneath his eyes, and I remember laughing afterwards, teasing him that he looked angry and mean when he came. I'm hot and flustered and signal to the girl that I'd like another drink, mouthing the words in the hope she can read my lips in the fading light.

My mind is playing a kind of elaborate game trying to spot any connections between the people I know here and the man I last saw in New Orleans a month ago. I rule out the Baxters straightaway and then I hear him behind me and I flinch, almost pushing Simon away.

'Penny?'

I spin around ungracefully.

'Oh my goodness. Craig? Simon, it's Craig.'

I have my hand on Simon's forearm. I can feel soft downy hairs and the hard ridge of scar tissue from the accident.

I am falling, spinning, not through air but what I imagine is a hot vacuum. Everyone seems to be looking my way and it's as if all of the heat and energy in the universe has been focused at me. The back of my dress clings to my skin along my spine and across my shoulder blades.

'Craig? It's you.'

I am scrabbling for something, like a burglar might in the drawer where I keep my underwear.

We met at a science conference in Bilbao where I was giving a paper. He made some joke about entanglement the following day as I woke in his hotel bed. Entanglement is a phenomenon that occurs when two or more objects are connected in such a way that they can be thought of as a single system. It had been the subject of my paper and his joke was lame, but I liked him, the way he frowned when I spoke, the way he made me feel.

That was in the spring of last year and I'd seen him several times since. 'Work,' I'd said to Simon who always believed everything I said. My phone had been ringing one time when we were at Craig's place in New Orleans. We'd

107

had dinner and I'd drunk quite a bit and when I picked up I told Simon that I was in Aspen and I had to jump in a cab to catch a plane to Salt Lake City and that I'd call him when I got there.

Afterwards I sat on Craig's settee nursing a large glass of brandy and marvelling at my ability to tell such an outrageous lie. I don't think of myself as capable of anything like that. I'm a leading figure in an obscure branch of quantum theory and my life's work is concerned with the search for certainties. I don't think of myself as a liar, a serial adulteress.

Craig said he thought I wanted to get found out. That deep down I was willing Simon to discover our affair, to drag it out into the open. But I really wasn't. I wished Simon wasn't so gullible, that he didn't take everything I said as honest and true. But I didn't want to get found out. It just wasn't worth it.

We were in Miami in an apartment that he'd borrowed from a friend. I was astride him and I can remember thinking how you couldn't tell which one of us was which. Our hair down there had become one and I know it sounds crazy but I didn't know who was inside who. It made me giddy then, my muscles vibrating at some special frequency, and I feel that again now, the eyes of the party on me, I think, and Craig at my side.

'Penny? Well I never.'

I imagine that everyone here, fanned out across the polished concrete, knows exactly what's going on. Like they've all seen this movie and are desperate to tell me that this is the good bit. The moment around which the whole plot hinges.

He's smiling at me, enjoying my awkwardness, his brow creased in anticipation of my next move. It's a playful frown and in another situation I'd find it extremely becoming.

'Craig Lawrence. It's good to see you.'

Everyone is looking at him, waiting for my introduction and I can hardly snatch a breath.

'Guys. This is Craig. He's another quantum nerd like me. Craig, this is Tim and Barbara, and my husband Simon.'

My eyes lock with his for a few seconds and I search them for a sign. He's smiling and frowning at me, inscrutable, and if I didn't know him better I'd think he was about to announce our affair or declare that he had no idea I was married.

'It's great to meet you. Penelope and I keep bumping into each other at conferences. Trying to outdo each other with claims about things nobody can see.'

He's already suggested an intimacy, a playful shorthand that, were he talking about someone else, I would suspect betrays a deeper connection.

Everyone says hi and Simon asks how he knows the Baxters.

'I'm doing work with Ted's firm. Quantum algorithms. Qubit interference. Turning shit off and on again.'

'You and Penny,' says Barbara, 'just amazing. Beyond my comprehension.'

It takes me a heartbeat to check if she's rumbled us already.

'I struggle with Excel. Really I do,' she says.

The girl brings me a fresh gin and tonic and asks the others if they'd like a refill.

109

Out in the paddock the horses seem agitated. A floodlight has come on and one tosses its head and whinnies.

I dread Simon saying anything and then he asks where's home for Craig.

'The Big Easy. Studied at Tulane and never left.'

The house is beautifully restored. Teak floors throughout and wonderful filigree ironwork on the balconies. Over one weekend last spring Craig and I did it in pretty much every room.

I play with the straw in my drink.

I know I need to be seen to be more involved. This is Craig, a work colleague, a collaborator, and we've run into each other at some random party out in the desert.

'This is incredible. That you're here.'

I've turned a quarter turn away from Simon and lowered my voice. Everyone can hear but I'm signalling that this is between the two of us.

'It is good to see you. I'm in shock.'

I lean towards him, my hand resting lightly on his sleeve.

'What are you doing here?'

My teeth are gritted in a way that makes clear I'm uncomfortable.

He's doing that thing that he does when he's listening intently. Smiling with his mouth, his eyes, but his brow suggests he's searching for something deeper. Some meaning perhaps.

'You working?'

'Just a couple of days. Ted invited me over and I thought why not? Never been out here before and he said he was having a party. I'm staying in the casita.'

He gestures back towards the house.

'Well that's great,' I say, for the benefit of the others, my eyes wide.

I know he must be loving this, watching me squirm. He's not mean or cruel but he has a sense of playfulness. The way he is with me when we're at a conference together. It's not quite flirting but it's familiar and in other circumstances makes me feel good, wanted, needed.

'So. How are you?'

I'm playing for time, filling some space in the hope that I can get him away from here, away from the others.

The horse whinnies again and then rises up on its hind legs, its front hooves flailing. I can see Ted Baxter passing his glass to the girl with the tray and making his way down the steps from the deck.

There is music like you might hear in an expensive bar. A satisfying beat, the melody a piano. Little speakers are concealed in the olive trees, like bird boxes. The conversation has stopped. Ours and the rest. Lydia is striding across the deck, after her husband. I think the floral print looks good on her and her shoes look expensive without being flash.

'It's good to see you, Penny. I wondered if you'd be here. Can't be many folk working on quantum theory in Santa Fe. I guess that's partly why I came. On the off chance.'

I stare at him, my eyes wide, pleading with him to shut up.

'I wanted to see you in your natural habitat.'

For a split second I have the urge to throw my drink in his face. I've never seen him like this, with people I know well, and I realise I've never really seen him at all. Apart from in various hotel rooms, or at his place, or perhaps occasionally with another colleague who I don't know well. But this is different. I'm with my husband, our friends, and he's being a dick.

Fortunately everyone's attention has turned to the commotion in the paddock. Both horses are agitated and one rears up followed by the other.

Ted is in the paddock and waving his arms like he's trying to bring a plane into a taxiway.

Lydia is with him and then running back towards us.

'Craig. Don't,' I whisper, deadly serious now.

Lydia heads into the house and we turn as one back to Ted. The horses are racing around the paddock.

'Mountain lion!'

Ted is waving his arms, the horses unsettled, circling the perimeter.

'Penelope?'

Craig is pretending to be affronted.

'I'm just pleased to see you, that's all.'

I still feel on edge. There is sweat between my shoulder blades and I sense a single drop running all the way down my spine. I'm glad of the commotion, the distraction.

Simon and Tim have peeled off and push through the throng of guests gathered at the lip of the pool. Lydia follows close behind from the house clutching a revolver and a cardboard box that I presume contains ammo.

'Wild West out here, ain't it?'

His accent is Southern and I'm not sure I've noticed that before. It makes him sound slow, a little unsophisticated, and I wonder if he's exaggerating it because he's here, in my world. He's standing too close and he needs a shower. There's something sharp about his smell, not stale but distinct, gamey.

'Please don't fuck this up for me, Craig. I'm serious.'

He's frowning again and I have absolutely no idea what he's thinking. It could be surprise, or confusion, or anger, or hurt or disgust. I just wish he'd go, leave me alone.

The three men are in the paddock waving and hollering. The horses are whinnying and making wide circuits at speed and under the floodlight I can see the big cat. Lydia is fumbling with the gun, and then hands it to Simon who fires two shots in the air. The sound echoes off the house and then disappears into the desert.

'Woah. Proper cowboy shit,' Craig whispers, his breath hot on my neck.

I can't see the mountain lion anymore but one of the horses runs at full tilt to the edge of the paddock and then leaps to jump the barbed wire but is caught. There is a gasp from the guests who are lined up along the rim of the pool.

'Fuck,' says Craig and darts off towards the paddock.

The horse has fallen awkwardly and is thrashing in the wire, making a terrible sound. The other one is still racing in a circle around the perimeter.

Lydia is screaming and the men seem frozen in a huddle. I can see Simon has the gun hanging loose at his side. He always says the Second Amendment will be the thing that eventually brings this country to its knees and I'm surprised to see him in the middle of everything, a weapon in his hand.

He's smart and kind and reliable and I feel calm when he's around. We've been together since college and he's been good to me, especially since my father died. He had a bad fall biking on a trail up in the mountains, concussion and the bone in his arm came clean through his skin, and although I wished it had never happened, I enjoyed nursing him. It knocked his confidence for a while but he's taken up long-distance running and I think he's better.

Craig has joined the others and they move as one to the perimeter where the horse is caught. Everything is lit by the ugly floodlight which makes the scene look unreal. Lydia's dress is blue and red and the colours pop against the featureless dust. She makes an attempt to grasp the running horse as it passes, but it dodges her, maintaining its panicked circuit.

Ted is trying to free the fallen horse from the wire and it kicks and catches him in the centre of the chest. Craig is there too with a blanket which he's wrapped around the wire. The horse's eyes are wild and sparkle like frost under the light.

Tim has his hand on Ted's back who's been winded but is still standing. Craig shouts something at Simon but it's lost in the sound of the horse crying out in pain. It's twisting and bucking, its legs flailing, and it flicks over onto its other side taking the wire with it.

Everyone along the pool edge is frozen, hands over mouths, silent.

There is spray coming from the horse's nostrils, and it thrashes again with its legs, a wild pedalling.

Lydia has cornered the other horse and it rears up again and again.

There is a slash of red on Craig's arm where he's been snagged by the wire. Ted is bent forward, his hands on his knees, Tim behind him, stock still. Craig yells at Simon.

'Shoot it!'

The horse is convulsing, frothing.

Simon is standing in front of the horse now, the revolver limp at his side.

'For fuck's sake, shoot!'

Craig has left the wire and I can see blood in the dust from the cut. He marches towards Simon.

'Gimme the gun!'

For a fleeting second I imagine Simon lifting his arm and shooting Craig in the chest. If he did, I think I'd love Simon forever and I would quietly carry my burden of guilt safe in the knowledge that it was an aberration, a madness that had thankfully passed.

There is an exchange, quieter now, and Simon hands Craig the gun. The horse is wild, its neck twisted awfully.

Tim and Ted have turned away. Lydia has the other horse by the halter and she's struggling to keep it calm. Simon is saying something to Craig who turns to look at him and nods silently.

He lifts the gun and fires three shots in quick succession.

Lydia screams and the other horse rears up and she loses her grip. Some of the guests have turned their backs, unable to watch. The rest of us are frozen. Simon and Craig stand in front of the horse, stilled now, its hooves twitching in the wire.

My mind is skimming over everything like a stone on a lake. The commotion in the paddock seems oddly distant, as if it's behind a screen. My husband is there, and a man I now realise I hardly know, with a gun.

I think back to that first time in Bilbao. The heat in my

chest when I'd felt noticed. He seemed so sure of himself, confident, and none of it had felt planned, like he was making a move. He was fascinated by my work. Genuinely impressed at what I was trying to do. And then I was face down on his bed in his hotel room and I felt like I was drunk on how fucked up everything had so suddenly become. How a world of precision and certainties and an attempt to understand how the smallest things in the universe might affect the nature of time and space itself, how all of that, and Simon, my husband of eighteen years, my rock, suddenly seemed devoid of meaning.

Later, when the dead horse has been covered with a tarpaulin, and the other one calmed, I sit with Simon and Ted and Lydia around a firepit. The dry wood cracks and pops, burning without smoke. We drink whisky in silence, staring into the flames. Someone has driven Craig to the hospital to get stitches. Lydia has stopped crying and looks glassy-eyed over the fire at me.

I smile weakly and I'm pretty sure she knows about me and Craig. Ted and Simon sit opposite each other across the fire, a mirror image, shocked.

I'm not sure what else could have been done. The horse was suffering terribly, in pain, frightened. And I'm not sure anyone will blame Craig for doing what he did. But I feel a dark fury towards him, an almost unbearable weight of anger at the man and what he's done.

I know it wasn't just him, that I was in control of my actions, the things I said and did. At any time I could have said no, refused to lie down with him. I was an equal in our affair and my deception is something I now must own but in this moment I can only see the fault is with him. It is this, the weight of my betrayal, the stink it leaves with me, that I feel so keenly. I have wandered so far from the person I thought I was and now I just want to be with Simon, to come home.

'I'm so sorry,' I whisper across the flames and everyone nods in return.

# Just to You

Jane Copland

He got the email alleging the misconduct at midday and had been prepared to drop everything. Her name didn't stand out to him, *Arianne*, although she said they had met earlier that year during a boat trip on the Thames from Hammersmith Bridge. A drinks event after a conference, it sank into the pile of forgettable outings with sweet beer and vinegary pinot grigio that attempted to be memorable but were always awkward and full of people squinting at each other's twirling lanyards. He remembered the evening only because he had gone on holiday the following morning, and in order to survive his 8 a.m. flight, he had made plans to leave the drinks function early.

*I don't know if you remember me*, Arianne said. *We met on the wharf and joked about how similar our names are. I attended your panel on women in higher education. I've kept this to myself but I can't help but feel like I need to say something.*

Adrian was no stranger to stories like Arianne's. He recognised the tone and probable subject matter immediately, and they always sparked a cocktail of purposeful dread and thrill in his gut as he prepared to take on a new case, a new righteous offensive. Through a decade of his early career, he had climbed the ranks of Human Resources at one of the country's largest engineering firms and had become incensed by HR's reputation for complicity in covering up bad behaviour. Case after case of harassment and abuse, both inside his employer's company and in the industry at large, reduced him to depression when they weren't making him scorchingly angry. He became indignant. He wouldn't stand for jokes that skirted even the outermost borders of being off-colour. In everyone who wasn't embroiled in an internal battle with their own anxiety, he saw people about to take advantage of those who were. His wife suggested a move away from HR as a profession given how much of a toll it was taking on him, and he'd agreed, moving back into academia and now on to his own venture. From his early years, he still prided himself on being an advocate for women and minorities.

He remembered the event, albeit vaguely. The boat trip from Hammersmith was meant to showcase the city but the evening had been misty and damp, despite it being late May. Most people crowded on the indoor lower deck, the air becoming as wet as it was outside and even smellier, ten hours of dress shirts and black coffee marinating in room-temperature lager.

Arianne said, *I joined a group conversation but I was way out of my league. I thought they were talking about partnerships between universities, which was why I stuck*

*around because that's what I do. But they were talking*
*about investing in businesses and engineering PhDs. I*
*didn't want to look silly by bowing out of a conversation I'd*
*sort of snuck into so I stayed. One of the people was Lewis –*

Adrian stopped reading. In the beginning, he'd taken full-
chested satisfaction in crashing down on the blackmailers,
the threateners and the creeps. He would go into bat, happy
to put an offender on trial and find him guilty after reading
one tweet, one text, one report. The offenders in question
were faceless and nameless after he'd dealt with them,
relegated to a scrapheap of subhumanity. The old-fashioned
days of science's and academia's pasts were clashing with
modern professionalism and he was happy to facilitate the
former's demise.

Arianne. Who is Arianne? He flicked to the bottom of her
email and clicked on the link to her Twitter account, noting
that she worked as an engineer and was based in Sydney.
He didn't recognise the long brown hair, grey blazer and
scooped off-white blouse. She looked older than he'd
expected and he was about to search for her on LinkedIn
before he was overcome by the dreadful, nauseous need to
keep reading. He didn't want to know. He never wanted to
read another word Arianne had written ever again. But he
had to know. She had said the name: *Lewis*. He wanted to
delete her email. Never got it. Caught in spam. Sorry, love.

*– was Lewis Bowden. He talked about his investment with*

*you. We had been in a group of six or seven but most people got off at Tower Bridge because on the way back, we were alone.*

Adrian had remembered more by then, mainly because he too had disembarked near Tower Bridge. He remembered the boat as well, a small river cruiser. The upper deck was outdoors with a wheelhouse and decorative funnel. It could have used several upgrades, notably replacement of the drab carpet, wood panelling and faded outdoor seating that had seen too many blustery Thames rainstorms.

*I didn't realise*, she said, *that everyone had gone.*

Adrian had met Lewis at an automation conference near Frankfurt five years earlier. There had been a speakers' dinner where Lewis waxed lyrical about his wife and twin daughters until midnight, when Adrian went back to the hotel and Lewis disappeared, seen next at lunch with a grey sheen and an ethanol-tinged odour. He was the personification of a hearty backslap: likeable, too easily forgivable, troublesome.

She said, *I didn't realise what was happening until we were down at the front of the boat. There was a funnel in front of the driver* (helmsman, Adrian thought) *and my back was against it. He pressed himself into me and put his hand behind me. I said I had to go and he kept talking about helping me, saying he could get me jobs and asking where I was staying. I told him I was staying with friends and he said I should come back to his.*

Adrian had never met Lewis's wife. It was unfortunate too, because he liked knowing the family members of people with whom he was going into business. She existed in the same ghostly fashion as many spouses: they were almost never seen in the flesh and if they were, it was awkward. He didn't know how old the twin girls were: Lewis had gone on about music or swimming or whatever, but they could have been five or fifteen. He found he was frantically chewing the inside of his bottom lip, creating a bloody ulcer that would be a weeping mess for days to come.

*I pushed him. It was noisy on the water and I didn't think it would make a difference to scream but I tried and he put his hand over my mouth. He grabbed my bum and shoved me against the funnel and kissed me and I threw my drink at him. I ran. I nearly fell down the stairs. I hid in the toilets until we got back to Hammersmith.*

There weren't any paragraph breaks until that point. Adrian found poor writing grating, unintentionally infantilising. Irritating. He glared, suddenly overcome by intense anger at the paragraph. Writing well was a poor skill to lack. He was angry at her for it. Made you look weak. Made her look weak. Maybe she was weak. Maybe he was. The anger smarted behind his eyes as the lip gave way and his teeth met in a tightly locked underbite, tasting of tart and salty flesh.

*I'm telling you this because I saw the press release about your upcoming launch and I couldn't stop thinking about what he did. I know I should have said something sooner and I apologise. I know that nothing ended up happening.*

*But I don't want it to happen to another woman.*

She signed off: Arianne, surname, Twitter link, foreign phone numbers. Kind regards. His lip wept.

Nothing happened. Happen again. She apologises. Another woman. *I'm telling you this because it happened.*

He'd heard so many stories before and he knew those stories were often widely shared under a cover of near silence, of near-blackout secrecy that sought to protect the injured but in fact did the opposite. They called it the whisper network. Many of the whispers were outwardly unremarkable, detailing folks who couldn't be trusted with early-morning speaking slots on account of their notorious hangovers, or who philandered but at least had the consent of the third party. But there were other stories too. Ones that were often never committed to text. Stories that mattered. Sweat blanched cold across his palms and forehead. He laid the question out, stretching it from one side of the office window to the other: had he ever heard anything about Lewis? Had there ever been an imperceptible nudge, a raised eyebrow, someone else's bitten lip, a nod in Lewis's direction that said *Wait, just a second, and listen for a whisper*. Years raced behind his field of vision; drinks, sighs, falters, stifled coughs, women politely exiting stage left before the evening's end. *I've got to go now*, flustered, in a hurry. Had he? And he decided, far too quickly and with far too much undue conviction, that he had not.

He had not. You haven't, Adrian. Promise me that you haven't.

*Help.*

Beyond the window, the bland skyline of Hackney wilted under August clouds. A lot had happened over the summer. There were six weeks left until the launch of his new company: a scientific research network in which interest from the academic sector couldn't have been hotter. Adrian had secured investment from four colleagues, three of them women. Three women, and Lewis. Before receiving Arianne's email he had been looking over the plans for the launch party. They were to rent the ground floor of the Hoxton Hotel and woo Silicon Roundabout for all its good fortunes.

He decided to talk to his wife, conducting the conversation in his imagination. In his head, his wife was appalled. She said, *Adrian, this is really bad. Did you know he was like this?*

*Promise me that you didn't.*

Lewis had gone through a number of jobs since he and Adrian first met, always managing to maximise either golden handcuffs or golden handshakes. He was leading research and development at a manufacturing conglomerate now; something in aerospace but with a consumer bent. He was always exceptionally busy and this was exemplified by lower-case, typo-ridden tweets that garnered positive responses and a lot of shares nonetheless. The need to write professionally somehow didn't apply to Lewis.

*

Adrian clicked on Arianne's company website and found a photograph of her with shorter hair and wearing those NHS-chic glasses that were making a bizarre comeback. His wife's face faded from his mind's eye and was replaced with Lewis's. He began the next imaginary conversation: clear the throat, steady the temper, light grimace.

*Lewis*, Adrian said to himself. *Mate.*

Backslap chat. It was a dialect they spoke to each other: a middle-class slang that combined plenty of *mates* with clipped Home Counties accents.

*Mate I've got an uncomfortable issue mate. Do you remember that seminar we spoke at a few months ago in Hammersmith? There was a boat trip?*

He stumbled in his script. Lewis would process the correct response before Adrian had got out the second *mate*. Lewis would know. Lewis always knew. *But I didn't*, Adrian thought. *Surely I didn't.*

*Oh*, Lewis would exclaim. *Yeah mate, I remember. Rain! Everyone sloshed!*

*There was a girl there, Australian?*

*Aaaahm?* Lewis's eyebrows met at a peak. Thoughtful, pious, home by dinnertime. *Wouldn't have the faintest, to be honest. Why, what's up?*

*She said you trapped her against the funnel and assaulted her.*

It wouldn't happen like that. In fact, Lewis wouldn't deny the memory.

*Oh . . . mate! Yeah I remember. She got hammered! I had to help her down the stairs. She spent the rest of the night puking but we got her a taxi in the end. She could barely remember where she was staying.*

Adrian could gently suggest that the undoubtedly *extremely* drunk Australian girl, whose version of events he *clearly* didn't buy, had implied Lewis had been too *friendly*; had made her uncomfortable. Lewis would look concerned, appalled even, that he may have been responsible for a moment of disquiet. He'd say, *Honestly mate I barely remember her. Extremely sorry if I caused offence?*

The investment would be safe but there would always be that cloud; that time Adrian mentioned that girl, Adrienne or something, who got drunk on that boat and made a scene. There would always be that exposed nerve between both of them, where Adrian saw Lewis and Lewis saw Adrian and the bar they leant against or the table across which they sat prickled and chilled. There would be that twitch of hesitation that Adrian, in every sense of the word, could not afford.

In future, he said to himself, he'd keep a closer eye on Lewis. It wouldn't happen again, not on his watch. Not to another woman. In fact, this was the best idea (he decided, alone in his head): it was vital to keep Lewis around. He was doing this to further the cause. He could help. He could build bridges, encourage change, keep watch, find a platitude that meant he didn't have to let go, not yet, a couple more years and a second round of funding . . .

Party plans back on the monitor, Adrian's gaze met Lewis's in the photo from the press release. With ten per cent more ownership of the new company than the other shareholders, Lewis stood in the middle of the group, hands around his co-investors' waists. On one tightly curled finger, his wedding ring glinted in the camera's flash, outshone only by his eyes.

*Don't you ever mention this, Adrian, especially not to me.*

If he dared to ask, the relationship was as good as dead. If he returned the money and fired him, Lewis would be free to roam. If he kept him close, Adrian could keep watch . . . *I'm doing this for her, really.* Adrian's mind strained at the equation of appeasing those glinting eyes, of deciding to do nothing. *I never got this email.* He closed the party plans. Even if Arianne's message was archived, and after his lip healed, never thought of again, he was still a saviour. Arianne who? Nothing happened really. Bit of a dust-up after too many beers. A misunderstanding most likely. She'll live. He silently wished her well. That was him; he was whole. A problem solved. A job well done.

# Flight Risk

Daniel Draper

**Joseph**

The first sign is the back pain, but I'm a man in my late thirties with a desk job so I think no more of it. I lie on my back on our living-room rug and my husband stretches my hamstrings and rolls my leg in case it's my sciatic nerve. I assure him it's not. He doesn't listen.

I tilt my head backwards and look at the radiator under the window. I've tried looking at the ceiling, but it needs a dust, and if I say anything it will become a Thing. I certainly can't look at Christopher. We haven't slept together in months. We haven't had any kind of sex in over twice as long. Neither of us has addressed it out loud. Christopher and I have been married five years. We love each other very much, but it's not working.

My spine cracks and there's a moment of relief. Intellectually, I know it's not my spine, but rather the bubbles of air in my synovial fluid. It feels like my bones. The pain isn't muscular. There's something wrong with my bones. I don't know how I know it's the bones, but it's the bones. I've tried explaining this to Christopher and I've failed to explain this to Christopher.

'While you're down there,' I joke. He does not laugh. But he does let my foot drop with a bang and mutters that he tried. His voice is gravelled and strained with a tight squawk. Nobody can say he hasn't tried, he mutters as he picks up his vape from the edge of the settee and heads out to the back yard. I stay lying down. The pain returns.

Even though I'm lying down flat I feel like I'm arching my back. The only comfort comes from being hunched over, so when the washing machine beeps, I get up and hunch. I look like a gargoyle that's got to do another full cycle, which I do, because there's double the bed linen.

I take two more ibuprofen from the kitchen cupboard on the way. It's only been an hour since my last two, but fuck it, let's live dangerously.

There's Saturday hubbub intruding on the kitchen. Neighbours' kids playing in their gardens, a lawnmower a few doors down. It's nice out. We're staying in. Saturdays are the worst. They have too much promise as the one day of the week where life needs to be lived. I hear the click hiss of that vape from Christopher followed by the infernal phup phup ah noise he makes smoking it. I empty the washer and put everything in the tumble dryer, because there's no way I'm pegging out with my back, no matter how gorgeous the weather gets.

He's on the patio. The patio we laid, stamping down any grass and mulch and worms that lived within the patch of Earth we scrimped and saved for. Why was this house such a symbol of 'making it' for us? Why was it so important to own a house? Some kind of safety? We'd moved back to Stoke because houses were cheap. We're locked into a mortgage with a term longer than we've been adults. I push away the thoughts that will give me a panic attack.

I watch his posture. He's also hunched, through habit rather than necessity, and typing on his phone with the vape in his hand. He used to properly smoke. My friends asked if it was like kissing an ashtray, which made no sense. Ash crumbles from the spent end of a cigarette. Cold and dead. His mouth was a warm, alive thing. It'd press against mine and I could feel him smile. The smoke was a comfort, like a roaring fire or the furnace of a kiln.

That thing he's huffing is supposed to taste like watermelon, but it smells like someone rubbed a watermelon over an air freshener. It catches at the sinuses where the roof of the mouth loops up into becoming nasal, and lingers. A grotty thing that makes me not want to kiss him. Well, that's what I'd say if he ever asked.

I switch on the dryer and it starts to whir and shake. Another machine. Like that damned vape. Everything needs plugging in and charging or powering up before it works. My throat constricts.

His sloped shoulders and defeated outbreaths break my heart. I want him to be happy. I almost wish he was having an affair, at least then he'd have something to look forward to. This slumped man is not the man I married. I've dragged him back here and it's killing him.

My slumped man is coming back in, and he looks like he wants to talk.

'Reckon it might be stress?' he asks, concern in his eyes.

Stress, he thinks. Course it's fucking stress. I check the timer on the tumble dryer and tell him I'm going to take a warm bath to loosen up.

'You using the posh bath stuff?' he asks.

I grunt in response. He just said it might be stress and now he starts on the bath salts? He can't look me in the face but he's keeping track of how often I'm using the fancy bath salts? I suppose they were a gift to both of us. Perhaps I ought to weigh them out equally and allot each of us our fair share?

I say nothing as I plug my phone into the socket on the wall, queuing up the whale song playlist to the wireless speakers in the bathroom.

I think unkind thoughts all the way up the stairs, each step hurting right above my coccyx. When I turn to give him a death glare, he's back on his phone as he rummages in the cupboard for cough syrup.

Nothing if not petty, I use two handfuls of the salts rather than one. Eventually, I submerge. When I'm in the bath, I feel weightless. No expectation to make anything right or work anything out, and it's not possible for me to do anything wrong. I keep my ears beneath the water to hear my own heartbeat, and even though I'm the most relaxed I've been all day my pulse is thrumming like a hummingbird.

**Christopher**

We're not even forty but to see us you'd think we were ninety. You'd think we were ninety but been dead since seventy. Saturday-afternoon baths? Googling about his bad back? This isn't what I thought marriage would be. I don't know how we got here and I don't know how we get out. I watch him walk upstairs to run a bath and he's walking funny. Buckled like he's doing an impression of a T. rex.

I glug the cough syrup and open the drawer for the emergency cigs. Real ones. I smoke one in the house. Fuck him. He knows full well I'm doing it, I could tell by the way his ire rose when I asked if he was having a long bath. His back's meant to be in agony, but he can still stiffen those shoulders. I refuse to let that man make me feel small.

Breath drawn in. Hold. Breath released. It's like meditation. If I said I need five minutes to myself I'd be sectioned, but a smoke break? Crack on. The only time I fully regulate my breathing is when I'm gulping down tar into my lungs. It's less the health risk that gets to me. It's the irony.

I breathe in again, but I can't seem to get a deep enough breath. It stops at my sternum, catches, and I have to breathe out again. I haven't said anything to Joseph, because heaven forbid anything gets in the way of him and his back. Besides, it'd be a bit rich to complain about shortness of breath when I'm literally stood in the dining room smoking. My throat feels constricted as well. The nub in my chest where my breath stops is caused by this marriage. My voice is going because I daren't use it to talk to him.

We eloped. It was stunning. Got a late ferry to Amsterdam from Newcastle, and workshopped vows on the way. It felt romantic and rebellious. We said words about being each other's anchors. Loads of nautical references because we're both smug clever fucks that know better than anyone else. In a way, we really have been each other's anchors. But I can't decide whether it's him or me that's the dead weight dragging the other down. Not that it matters. Either way we both drown. I hate how maudlin

I've become.

I stub out the cigarette and open the window, pretending it will make a difference as I listen to the battering of the tumble dryer.

**Joseph**

I don't know how long I've been in the bath. I'm finally roused by the smell of Christopher cooking dinner downstairs. Grilled fish and seasonal vegetables because we're trying to be healthy. We decided this over an animated discussion on how we don't feel like ourselves, completely avoiding the real reasons. He wants to get rid of the paunch he's developed. I've convinced myself my impotence will be cured by cutting out saturated fat.

The bath hasn't soothed my back at all. The only relief I feel is when I arch out and bend my knees. The backs of my legs feel like they're shrinking. I shuffle my way downstairs, trying not to lift my feet too much. When I get to the kitchen I can see Christopher's been crying. I know every line on his face and every subtle change in pallor. His face is becoming pinched and stern. I wonder if he's caught something glandular. I used to watch him sleep, and the tidal rise and fall of his breath would calm me. I'd lie next to him and hold my own breath for fear he'd wake up and see me for what I was, realise his mistake and bolt for the door. Maybe that's the problem, now he really has seen me.

'Smells good,' I say.

'Babe, you look like shit,' he replies, far kinder than it sounds when I repeat it. I walk over and nuzzle my head under his chin, even though I'm taller than he is. He's warm. I'm stooped. He puts his arm around me and kisses the top of my head. 'Just tell me what you need,' he says, and I feel the strength it's taking for his voice not to crack.

I don't mean to sound facetious, I really don't. When I reply, I'm being more honest than I've ever been in my entire life.

'I need to see the sea.'

## Christopher

He really does look like shit. To the point where I consider ringing 111. I've spent the afternoon with earphones in, cleaning and trying to block out that sodding whale song Joseph likes when he has a bath. How anyone can find it relaxing is beyond me. But this is it. Saturday afternoons. Light hoovering, a sweep and a mop of the parquet floor in the kitchen, and the endless not quite quiet of the suburbs. I'm not breathing right, so I take some of our mouth tape and fasten it across my lips for the afternoon to force me to breathe through my nose. I'd read somewhere that nasal breathing can cure a multitude of health issues, but we'd got the tape to stop him snoring. Strange how much I'd love to hear him snore now.

For a while I was convinced he was cheating. I'd gained a little weight, he'd become withdrawn and uninterested. He'd always been shy, but never uninterested. He'd had a quiet intensity of attention to him for as long as I've known him. Shrewd and noticing.

The mouth tape doesn't work, so I try some nasal strips and stick two to my nose to clear the airways as much as possible. It doesn't occur to me then that they're too big for two to fit on one nose, but my mind is occupied with him upstairs.

I'm not proud of myself, but I sneak through his phone, making sure I don't accidentally pause his horrendous whale noises. I see the search history for Viagra, testosterone supplements, and even enquiries about a sexual support therapist. I think back to our engagement. How the mighty have drooped. And that's where the problem lies, isn't it? He doesn't trust me. He can't talk to me. I put the phone back on charge and cry through the best part of half a pack of cigs before starting dinner.

Hours pass and he's hobbled over to the kitchen table, and it's not just my breathing that feels laboured. It's the entire bottom of my face. I rub my neck and cheeks for any specific areas of pain, but it's more like a sinus headache. If my sinuses were in my jaw.

We eat. We barely speak. I've lost my appetite and can't stomach this bland nonsense we're putting ourselves through, but he's wolfing down cheap hake as if it were gourmet. At first I think he's taking the piss, or performing to try and make me feel better, but no. He becomes animated in a way I haven't seen in a long time. Frenzied. Truth be told, I'm furious. I know how much he despises our little health kick, but I'm trying to show willing and move forward.

After dinner we sit in front of the TV with this cracked marriage hovering above us. I decide not to bring up the impotence. He thinks I don't notice, like I'm too thick to see when the man I love is upset. It makes it harder for me to breathe. I hate him for it, then console myself that hate like this is the corollary of love. I hate that even after all this time he'd be surprised I know what the word corollary means.

He says he feels weak and is going to bed early.

I say goodnight through the bile caught in my throat.

His cryptic shit before dinner about the sea has wound me up. He wants to go to the sea. It was his idea to move here, not mine. I would have been perfectly happy living out by the North Sea as we always had done. No, we moved. We told ourselves the move was the only way we could afford a house, but I know the real reason was to be closer to his family. The family we don't even see.

I'll not be dragged down into bitterness. If he wants the sea, then we'll go to the fucking sea. We live a decent ninety-minute drive from a beach so we'll have to get an early start.

I'm trying, I swear to God I'm trying.

I don't realise that I've fallen asleep on the settee until I wake up.

I hear snaffling from the kitchen that sounds like a fox has got in. Rabid and animalistic. I walk in and I see the fridge door open, lighting him up in his boxer briefs as he leans over the worktop, contorted in the way I now consider his. I see the problem with his back. The bones are wrong, like his ribs have migrated to his back and a slight, but definite, tailbone has ruptured the skin.

The noise is sloppy and joyous, and his arms are pinned to his sides as he tucks in. I turn on the big light to really see what he's doing. He's using his mouth to peck at the rest of the raw fish in its polystyrene tray. I choke down a gag at the globs of slimy white juice running down his chin and flecks of flesh around his lips when he whips his head around. He has a sickening grin on his face.

'Sea?' he asks with childish wonder. 'Now?'

**Joseph**

I don't understand the horror on his face. Isn't sushi just raw fish? And besides, it was his idea to watch what we eat anyway. Less oil if we don't cook it. Ha. My eyes feel sharper. I've stopped trying to fix my posture. I've stopped trying to fix his posture. Let him stand like that, leaning over the countertop with his head in his hands. I resist the urge to caw at him. I carry on with the fish. It's cold. I'm not chewing it properly and feel the chunks of flesh as they hit my stomach.

'Joe –' he says.

'Christopher,' I snap back. 'Will you take me to the sea or not?' I don't mean to be cruel. I still love him very much, but he's a fool. He doesn't notice things. It's the good looks that have done it. He's not pretty as such, but has a classically handsome air, a sense of majesty. Or he used to. One of those men who felt safe and secure. Not a man for a wild passionate affair, but he'd never run off with my pension either, though sometimes I wish he would. Show some spine. Ha. I can feel my spine. It really is wrong.

I snatch glances at him as I eat. He's changing, starting to look long in the mouth, as if his teeth are clumping into one long outwardly protruding fang. He's becoming beaky. I grunt and tap my foot on the floor.

'You'll get food poisoning, you stupid twat,' he says as he grabs me and tells me to make myself throw up. I imagine what it would be like to peck him to death, and it's not until I've shoved him away from me that I realise I've got a full erection. Ha.

I stop stooping. I bolt up to my full height. The muscles

in my legs completely detach, but I don't feel any pain. In an instant, the metatarsals in my feet have grown as long as a shinbone, and for a moment I tower over him. Then there's a crunch. I'm a bird. I'm a man. I'm Diogenes' featherless biped. Ha.

I still have my broad, flat nails on my fingers and toes, but these will go soon. My ankles are high and snapped backwards. My arms are pinioned to my sides. My thighs and upper arms are shrinking into my body. I don't have feathers yet, but they're coming. I can feel them pushing against my goosebumped skin, ready to burst through. I shriek at Christopher.

He grimaces. I know that he's going to be sick before he does. I can smell it leave his stomach and travel up his throat. It leaves his beaky-looking mouth and sloshes on the floor in front of me. I shriek again and step forward, feeling undigested broccoli between my toes. Never chews his food. Wasteful. I try and scream this, but all I manage is a caw. The pain I've had has gone. I lean down to eat the mess he's made on our floor and notice the ease in my joints and the smooth swoop of my body that takes my face into the warm fishy goop he's served for the second time that night. I lap it up gratefully.

**Christopher**

I can't watch it. I just wanted to feel safe. A nice home, a nice husband. A nice life. I've ended up making a prison.

I bound up the stairs and rinse my mouth out and find it changed. I've got a beak. I clack my teeth together and they're not there. It's a fucking beak. My breath still comes in shallow bursts, and my tongue feels thinner and more mobile in my mouth. My temporomandibular joint clicks but still moves. I practise speech. A E I O U. The sound isn't human anymore, but my brain seems to be working. My hoovered-up knowledge from old *ER* episodes seems to be as sound as it ever was. I can feel where my nose cartilage is hardening into bone and the skin of my upper lip is thinning out as it becomes speckled with yellow and black. The pit of my stomach is dropping as my centre of gravity shifts, and the need to be in the sky and free thumps through every part of my body.

My chin has receded and I swear my eyes are moving out from where they were this morning. What was my greying five o'clock shadow has turned to rich black down.

**Joseph**

I can't knock on the door with my hands because I don't have hands anymore. I need the sea. If he ever loved me, he'd see. Ha. CC him in on this urgent message, you see? The sea. Ha. Sea. Seaseasea. My fingers have fused together and the range of motion in my arms doesn't work in a way I understand yet, so I scratch at the door with my feet. My three-toed, newly webbed feet. I need the sea. Sea.

**Christopher**

I let him in the bathroom. He's shrunk. A four-foot-tall Thing peers at the mirror and we note that our transformations are not equal. His body is nearly entirely bird in structure, but still encased with skin. He still has his wonderful human face. I look at myself and see that my entire head and neck are that of a cormorant. My body, though still human, is feathered.

He can speak. I cannot.

He needs the sea. I need sky.

**Joseph**

Sea. Seaseasea. Sea. I raise my not-hand to where his face used to be, but it's so far away. My arm is beautiful though. White feathers stream out and stop abruptly at the elbow. I can't fly yet. But I will. The sea. Ha. Caw. Sea.

**Christopher**

I peck at his wing to calm him.

'The sea?' he asks. I nod. I haven't felt so sure of anything since we moved in together. I can do this for him. I can give him what he needs. What we both need. Catching sight of my plumage in the mirror I realise I don't need my voice. I need wings.

His skin is greying and becoming dimpled over his now scrawny legs and torso. What were his chest and ribs have fully barrelled out into a bird shape. The feathers only begin on his wings. Each time I turn away the feathers increase. My hearing's keener than it's ever been, and I listen to the light ping of fingernails hitting the tiles as they rip from their nail beds, pushed out by the stretching skin and furrowed down that's sprouting.

He's becoming shorter.

We're going to drive. I bundle him downstairs. If we're going to end up as birds, I pray that my hands and legs don't change before we get to the coast.

I can already feel my brain shrinking inside my new

skull.

When we leave the house I don't bother locking the door. It doesn't seem important anymore. I consider writing a note for whoever finds the empty house, but it'd probably be weeks. Jesus Christ it'll probably be work that sounds the alarm. How depressing.

I shake my new neck as I close the door and fight the urge to leap into the cold night air. Not that it's hard to fight, given I don't have wings yet. I lean down and rub my head against Joe's back to nudge him forward. He hops confidently down the path to the passenger side of the car and slaps the door with what is now a full wing. His feathers catch the light from the streetlamp. He is beautiful.

I open the door and he hops in, small enough to sit loaf-style on the seat. A human head on a bird body, he looks grotesque. A chimera. A suburban answer to the sphinx, the lion body swapped for a seagull. Not that the sphinx ever took the passenger side in a Ford Mondeo. And even if it did, at least the riddles of the sphinx had an answer.

I start the car.

### Joseph

Smell. I'm smelling everything. I try telling Christopher, but he can't respond. His voice has disappeared, replaced with clicks and caws, but I still have my human head. Even though I'm sat, I can feel myself shrink, feathers sprouting all over my body. By the time we leave the A41 at Chester I smell where he's taking me. Rhyl. Ha. I flutter my wings in appreciation, but I don't think he notices. My wings have greyed, but the feathers sneaking across my body are still bright white.

I look at him and he's still big. Human-sized. But he's also feathered. His feathers are black, and there's a majesty in his transformed neck and face. His arms are still arms. His legs still operate the pedals.

The sea. My God how I want to swoop over the sea. I stretch my wings to their full span to test them, imagining how strong I'll be as I dive and fish. He slaps my wings down and caws at me in a way I know means to pack it in.

I oblige.

## Christopher

We're about forty minutes away. I didn't notice the border into Wales but we must have crossed it because the signs are bilingual. I'm not scared. I'm not even worried. Whether I'm having a psychotic episode or there truly are tailfeathers growing out between me and the seat, there's a sense of relief.

It takes more effort to reach the pedal. I shuffle forward and slam my foot down on the accelerator as my fingers begin fusing together.

The sea. I can't be a bird before we get to the sea. There's a flash of light from a speed camera, not that they matter anymore. What are they going to do? Revoke my licence? I laugh out loud and it comes out as a squawk. I imagine the DVLA sending a fine back to the house. I imagine the human reader's face as the letter's opened to an image of a man-sized cormorant driving with a seagull sitting politely beside him. My laugh comes out as staccato caws into the pre-dawn light.

**Joseph**

It's sunrise behind us when we stop. Christopher's been shrinking and changing for the last dozen miles. Thank God we're on an empty road when the car stalls.

I flap. I rear up and I flap. We're trapped in the car with no way out. Bound not by our marriage, our mortgage, our jobs, but by a simple car. I scratch at the dashboard until Christopher, now a sleek and terrifying cormorant next to me, pecks at the electric-window switch on the driver's side and lithely slips through the widening gap. I follow, stopping to look at myself in the wing mirror and seeing a full seagull's face reflecting back at me.

Christopher stands at the side of the road with his eyes focused on me. Dignified. My husband, the bird. His plumage is mostly black except for a grey breast that turns into a multitude of browns down his middle. He spreads his massive wings and preens.

Typical. He turns into a stalwart of the sea. I turn into a chip-botherer.

He caws. He stamps. He's upset. He beats his wings as he stands on the verge, trying to communicate something to me that I don't understand.

I jump up and fly towards the beach.

**Christopher**

Arsehole. Even when we're literal birds he can't understand me. I jump up and join him in flight.

**Joseph**

As soon as I'm in the air I realise my human brain never understood the sky. In the sky? Entirely the wrong preposition. Of the sky, or through the sky. It's been a long night. I become hungry. Ravenous. Ha. As a human, I'd get dizzy at heights above ten feet, but now I'm manoeuvring and whirling, ascending, bombing down to scavenge litter and then catching up with Christopher. He's flying very high and very straight. He's homing in on the coast. I'm playing.

**Christopher**

He doesn't get it. Cockerels blast their noise into the air and we join the chorus. I see Joseph looping beneath me, dancing on the eddies of wind as they rise above the streets where slowly, humans are beginning their Sundays.

**Joseph**

We see the sea.

**Christopher**

We see the sea.

**Joseph**

A flock of seagulls are stuck to the edge of the coast. They swirl and swoop and strut along rocks. They scavenge. I scavenge. He doesn't.

**Christopher**

We stand on a rock and look at each other, truly. I want to thank him. I want to tell him I love him. I caw.

**Joseph**

I want to thank him. I want to tell him I love him. I caw.

**Christopher**

I bow my head. I let go of the last things that make me human.

**Joseph**

I bow my head.

I wonder if some magpie will find our wedding rings left in the car. Thieving gits.

**Christopher**

I take to the northern sky.

**Joseph**

I take to the western sky.

**Christopher**

My wings stretch.

I soar.

# Ingredients

Richard Hooton

The mackerel stares glassy-eyed from the slab, thin skin translucent, downturned mouth open gormlessly. I know how it feels. I chose a seat at the chef's table so it wouldn't be obvious I'm here alone. A table for two can feel desperately large and lonely since Mandy left me. I shuffle on my tall stool. I'm too high up, too on show, too precariously balanced.

No menu; so I guess, same as life, I'll get what I'm given. A thick piece of card on the marble counter bears an explanation in a fancy font: 'Welcome to Where Memories Crystallise. We work directly with farmers, fishermen and foragers from soil to shore to get the freshest, finest ingredients, enhanced by our culinary excellence and creative touch. Just as an author uses all five senses to evoke a story, we do the same to craft a unique, sensory experience that brings lasting memories.'

Conversations bubble and burst around my silence. I brave a glance around. An open-plan, former coffee warehouse, the beehive-busy kitchen on show. Huge windows framing the rooftops outside and filling the high-ceilinged space with light. Shabby chic with bare brick walls, wooden beams and distressed furniture. A hipster hangout. Blokes with beards trimmed square like upturned hedges sit at Ercol tables. I've not seen men wearing braces to hold up their trousers for decades. My faded-blue jeans stretch around an ever-expanding waist, my polo shirt just covering my beer belly. I rub a scuffed shoe on the back of my calf.

Lads at the depot would never come somewhere like this. Didn't even tell my mates down the pub where I was going. They don't know my older brother's a Michelin-starred chef. Even when they were chatting about this trendy new place and how their other halves were desperate to book, I never piped up. They all mocked it.

Not my kind of place either; it's five times what I'd fork out on a meal. Good job it's Gordon's treat. The emailed invitation, cursory and cautious, came out of the blue. I'm only here out of curiosity, to see what my brother does and how easily he's able to rip people off. Pretentious tosh, taking advantage of folk with more money than sense. Food's just food, eaten to keep you going. Give me a steak and ale pie any day or a Friday fish supper or a spag bol when out with Mandy at an Italian for our anniversary.

I see him striding forward in his clean, crisp, chef whites. My stomach pancake-flips. Same crooked nose, square jaw and thinning thatch that've descended the Compton male line. He halts yards from me. No eye contact, but he knows I'm here. Sat waiting. Flicks of his wrist have staff dancing to his tune as to a conductor. Barked orders, that deep voice still coated in gravel.

A decade-old memory surfaces. Gordon centre stage,

delivering the eulogy, being fêted by everyone. He barely involved me, sitting on the outskirts, an observer at my own father's funeral. It needled; and, with the occasion, the emotions, I admit I lost it, telling him what I thought of him, how he always had to be the big man, how it was always about him. Some memories are so seared into the brain that they still burn. We've barely spoken since. This, the closest we've been in all that time. Both parents gone now, the glue that bound us dissolved. He's the only family I have left.

'Hi, Phil.' I'm startled by a waitress greeting me as breezily as a best mate. So, he's told them about me. 'I'm Kate. I'll be serving you today.'

I grunt. Slip of a lass, sparrow-like, probably only ever pecks at salads. Her bleached-blond pixie haircut emphasises her angular face. She's wearing denim dungarees over a black top; hardly a uniform.

'An aperitif.' Kate slides a tumbler across the counter as if its lurid content is precious. A sip. Just poxy fizzing fruit juice. I give her a glare. I could murder a good pint; need something to take the edge off. I'm supposed to be having wine to match the meal. 'Our homemade, sparkling blood-orange drink.'

I knock it back.

A hush descends as if we're in a theatre with the play beginning. Midsummer rays scatter through the window, a warmth from behind, as though the sun's shining directly onto my back. Birdsong warbles above.

Kate presents me with an auburn plate so rustic it might have been found in a farmer's field. 'A Woodland Wander,' she whispers.

Nothing to it, a simple salad with nuts and whatnot. I was right, just a con.

Kate hands over a cool glass of white wine. I take a swig, let the alcohol do its easing.

I'm too hungry not to eat. I pierce a forkful of jagged-edged, paper-thin leaves, scoop up some toasted hazelnuts, spike a sliver of mushroom and pop it into my mouth. Rustling springs from somewhere, the crunch of foliage under foot, wood pigeons cooing. A scent of soil and pine, woody and sweet. Brittle leaves combine with the mushroom's creamy softness. Another mouthful: salt-baked beetroot's earthiness, a pungent heat from wild garlic flowers. Something stirs inside me. Buttery-soft roasted chestnuts, peppery rocket, bitter dandelion leaves. Lush greens and golden browns. That warmth on my back, a gentle breeze, the birdsong intensifying.

A long-forgotten memory unlocks from a brain cell. I'm in between my dad and brother, hand in hand, being swung high, feet skimming ground then air. I'm five, maybe six, the giant trees of Delamere Forest all around.

As I eat, the memory is a butterfly I'm struggling to pin down, fluttering away as my fork clinks onto an empty plate. Willing it back, I'm left grasping at fog.

I spy Gordon watching me, knife gleaming in his hand. He quickly focuses on his task, sliding the blade behind the mackerel's gills then severing the top of its spine to remove the head. He separates flesh from bone with subtle slices. The speed and skill are extraordinary; he's a surgeon in his precision, an artist. The fish is rapidly carved into neat, rectangular portions, not a scrap of waste. It's rare to sit and watch someone work. Folk can tell you what they do for a living, and you might know what that entails or picture them in action, but seldom do you get to see them sweat and toil close up. Gordon seasons the mackerel and I've got to hand it to him, he knows what he's doing. Still, he's always been dedicated to his career, no hobbies or social life, little time for anything else. It's been easy to avoid him. Though I've read all his reviews.

I'm satisfied with my job on the buses, driving the familiar routes, the same stops, exchanging a few pleasantries with the regulars. I'm on autopilot these days, don't have to think too much or take anything home, just clock on, clock off.

Gordon puts a pan on a hob and turns up the heat. Pours in some oil that hisses. A perfect rectangle of fish is fried and within seconds placed in a deep-bottomed, aqua-blue bowl that's swapped with my plate. The mackerel rests in a green pool.

'Fishing for Supper,' says Kate. 'Enjoy.'

Water is trickling somewhere, starts to flow. Eau de lake: oily fish, bulrush and willow. I taste the flaky white meat, lemony, zesty as the sun, that warmth still massaging my back.

A memory, bonfire-hazy, coquettish in its unveiling. A rowing boat, I think, bobbing in the middle of a lake, swaying rhythmically, water sloshing the sides. My dad and brother again, fishing rods gripped, lines disappearing into the depths. Trees in the background. I'm certain it's connected to the previous reminiscence, maybe later in the day.

A yelp of delighted surprise. Dad encouraging as Gordon's fingers frantically reel in a catch, the fish flapping through the air into the boat's concavity. Slaps on the back from Dad, who then drags aboard his own whopper. Gordon revelling in more catches, Dad only just outshining him.

My line remains slack in the water. Cast again and again, desperation surpassing hope. Stinking fish writhing in the hull, gaping mouths mute as mine. An emptiness in the pit of my stomach. Dad calls it a day, hails their triumph. I hide my face as he rows us back.

I snap free. Now I know what Gordon's up to; a smugness detected in his sly smile. He's conjuring these memories to rub my face in his superiority as easily as rubbing herbs into fresh meat. A gulp of wine, acidic on my tongue. Gordon was always the first to everything. To get a girlfriend, a job, a car. Success comes easy to him.

I'm ready to storm out but I know how it'll look and I don't want to give him the satisfaction. The other diners seem spellbound.

I sample a spoonful of broth, garlicky, the heat of ginger, a powerful punch in complete contrast to the delicate fish. Parsley and tiny shoots float like duckweed and water hyacinth in the murky liquid. Daylight's fag end dims. A coldness shivers me. I close my eyes.

I remember the early-morning chill, the grey sky. Sneaking from the tent as they snore, fishing rod in my hand. Sitting on the edge of the wooden jetty. Leaning forward to focus on something drifting by. Losing my balance, panic spiralling through me, toppling headfirst, the shock of the icy water, its foulness filling my mouth, my lungs, as I gasp as uselessly as those fish. Darkness. A sinking anvil. Arms churning. Flailing feet tangled in thick weeds and rushes that claim me for the lake bed.

Dull shouting, splashing. Hands grabbing my armpits, hauling me upwards, breaking the surface, dragged back to oxygen and light. Both of us lying on the jetty, spluttering so much we can't speak. We look at each other as dawn breaks, my brother raising a hand, forefinger and thumb meeting in a perfect circle. I match it with my own shaky sign.

In waterlogged socks and dripping clothes, we traipse back to the tent leaving puddles in our wake. Our gobsmacked father swathes us in towels next to a roaring campfire until feeling returns to lifeless limbs. He scolds me for going off without them, for being so reckless.

I open my eyes. Down the wine. Gordon has never brought up the time that he saved me. I'd always thought that muddy recollection was just a recurring nightmare, less real with each rendition. There's solidity to the memory now. And the stony realisation that I've been cautious ever since.

My brother strips meat from Bugs Bunny's carcass. I don't even need the additional senses stimulating to see the image of our father skinning and gutting a rabbit he'd snared then cooking it in a pot over the campfire to serve with beans. Is that where Gordon got his culinary skills from? He got all of Dad's best aspects.

Gordon lays the meat tenderly in a slick frying pan and

it sizzles and shrinks as it sears. He shunts it into an oven. Rescues it after a short while, then lets it rest.

Dusk is descending. The industrial lights dim too. An invisible fire crackles, smokiness hanging in the air.

'A Snared Jumper.' Kate appears from nowhere to serve the course: hearty meat, smoky and astringent, the macho flavours getting on like old comrades, on a bed of broad beans, smoked bacon lardons, carrot, onion and celery. A glass of red wine, strong and heady. Everything soon gone.

Kate swoops, seizing my empty plate and glass. 'All good?'

I nod tentatively.

The lights go out, plunging us into pitch black. Gasps seem to slurp the air from the room. A chill slithers, tendrils of dread snaking inside me. It's difficult to acclimatise, to hear my ragged breathing, to be left so vulnerable. Deathly quiet is pricked by the odd owl hoot and swept by swishing branches.

The tent's canvas billows and sways in the dead of night. Forehead and hands clammy despite the cold. Panting, heart racing, uncertain where I am, in this field in the middle of nowhere. The nightmare beneath the lake ringing in my mind.

A hand gently touches my shoulder, then guides my arm forward. Am I inside the tent or the restaurant? Black becomes grey. My fingers meet a hot, porcelain mug and find its handle. I lift it to my lips, steam skimming my face, and sip velvet smoothness that coats my tongue in bitter dark chocolate, luxuriant and comforting. Is it Kate or Gordon at my side?

My brother holds me, tells me where I am, that I'm safe, that he's here. He makes me hot cocoa by the campfire and we sit in silence until my heart resumes its regular rhythm, my brow is dry and I can close my eyes again.

The lights come back up. A wave of palpable relief washes the restaurant, a few nervous giggles and muttered comments.

'Final course.' Kate places a glazed ceramic dish and a dessert wine in front of me. 'Sheep's milk ice cream with honeyed yoghurt. Or what we call A Frozen Fleece.'

The scent of freshly mown grass. Lambs bleating in a far-off field. The creamiest ice cream I've ever tasted with a tangy syrup drizzled over it. Sweet scoops of carefree childhood bliss. I'm not sure if the wine's gone to my head but a mellowness bathes me, macerated as a strawberry soaked in rum.

I'm transported back to the final morning of our camping trip, perched with Gordon on a fence by a meadow, licking the last drips of our 99s from sticky hands. Gordon suggests a blood pact to ensure we'll always be there for each other. He produces from his rucksack the knife Dad used to skin the rabbit. With gritted teeth and a deft flick, he slices his palm, blood trickling like raspberry sauce.

Gordon hands me the knife. I hesitate. Don't want to back out or let him down. I feel the stinging blade rip my skin, biting my bottom lip to stop myself crying out. Gordon clasps my hand, mingled blood dribbling onto dew-fresh grass.

I lift my right hand, spreading my fingers. The slightest trace of a scar along my palm, as though a raised life line. My dessert is melting. I savour each spoonful, then sit back, satisfied, bursting with long-buried memories magically revived.

We make unbroken eye contact and I see the boy who cared for his younger brother. The meal, the memories, a bridge between us. Gordon raises a hand, forefinger and thumb meeting. I mirror his gesture. A smile spreads across my sibling's face like butter on hot toast. Tears cloud my eyes, are blinked into clearness.

Kate takes my dish. 'How was it?'

'Delicious. Worth every penny.' I smile broadly. 'I'll give my compliments to the chef.'

# The Anonymity of a Seaside Town in Winter

Helen Kennedy

Seasons are unhinged in seaside towns. Places where the tide comes in and goes out and no one asks questions. In the flat white of winter, the high street is paralysed with shut-up shops. The aluminium-grey sea drags at the rim of gravel. The sound she hears in her head when she isn't remembering. When the sea is anonymous. Forgiving.

She steps into the water, the cold under her skin, seeping between organs and tendons and inflated lungs. She likes the weight of it in her hair, the pull of the tide. Her salted eczema tightens and stings. As a child she'd been afraid of the water, but now it's where she can be disconnected. Unknowable. She swims against the tide, away from the Cobb. In the distance, Charmouth sits like an open mouth in the estuary and the cliffs at Black Ven shadow the beach. Rockfalls of debris reach into the sea, landslides of Liassic clay dislodged by the winter storms. People come to the coast here to find fossils, to unbury the past.

The sea always wipes the slate clean.

The Blue Tit Swimming Club ladies congregate next to the

groyne in dry robes, and their high-pitched voices carry across the beach. They peel off layers like skin and put on wetsuits, neoprene hats and bootees. She keeps her distance as they swim to the buoy, their heads like grey seals amongst the breaking waves. They ask too many questions.

Tomorrow she'll take the bus to Axminster and Jimmy will want to know what work she's applied for, where she's living. He always swallows too hard before he speaks, makes notes in an A5 notebook even though it's really a tick-box exercise. Jimmy isn't a parent, and it shows.

There are always children in seaside towns. In places that cling to the cliffs, moving between schools that don't ask too many questions. Her daughter Shelley used to love the beach, the bright sunshine on her face, filling up buckets with seawater. In the galloping summer, the town is thick and tight with tourists digging for bones. The streets sticky with ice cream and chip-shop ketchup. Bins overflowing with lager cans. The iridescent blur of blue sky. In the high season everyone is a stranger. She likes that freedom.

She dries herself quickly after she's stepped out of the water, pulls on warm clothes and a hood against the wind. Her hair is plastered salt hard against her skull. She stares into the distance. The Blue Tit ladies are circling arms and calling like gulls, heading back to the beach. Their voices carried on the wind.

On the promenade, a little girl with ammonite eyes is pulling on her mother's sleeve. But the mother is ignoring her, talking into her mobile phone and sucking on her cherry vape. The little girl's voice is high and whiny like a cat. She remembers Shelley making that sound. The mother sucks on the vape and blows it into the cold circling air. She watches the little girl drag her feet. She'd like to pick her up and give her a cuddle, feel her warm breath on her face.

She stops for coffee at the café kiosk, her cold hands fumbling for change in the bottom of her swim bag.

'You here for the winter then, are you?' the man behind the counter says. She nods.

She takes her coffee and sits by the window where she can watch people walk up and down the seafront. The man behind the counter is watching her closely, his silver-shine hair and slippery-mackerel mouth. She sips her coffee, turns away, but he's still watching the back of her head.

The mother comes into the café. Her little girl with ammonite eyes is screaming now, her face raw with tears. The mother isn't paying her daughter any attention, she's playing with her hair, twirling it round her fingers. Talking animatedly into her mobile phone, wedged under her thick chin.

'I want an ice cream,' the little girl says.

The mother orders a black coffee and a strawberry milkshake, and they come and sit at the table next to her. She watches the little girl suck the thick pink liquid through a straw, her cheeks puffing in and out. The little girl has hair that falls in soft blond curls. She'd like to sit her on her knee and smooth her hair with her hands. Smell her soap-washed skin. The mother tears open two small packets of sugar and stirs them into her coffee. She continues to scroll

159

through her phone feed.

Suddenly the mother gets up and says, 'I'm going to the lav, can you watch her a minute?' She's already walking across the café, but the little girl hasn't noticed.

'Yes,' she says, and turns her chair towards the little girl who is still sucking at the straw. She notices that the girl has blue shining eyes, strawberry cheeks.

'What's your name?' she asks the little girl.

'Courtney.' She can feel her throat tighten, these silly made-up names, celebrity-type names. She scratches at her eczema arms. 'Do you like ice cream, Courtney?' she asks. The little girl nods. She leans forward and slides her arm around her waist, the smell of her jasmine hair and soft cheeks. When the mother comes back from the toilet, Courtney is sitting on her knee, but she doesn't seem to notice this. The little girl feels as light as a feather, as light as a memory.

'She reminds me of my daughter when she was little,' she says to the mother, giving Courtney a squeeze. Her small body is soft and squidgy. Comforting.

The sea breathes in and out.

Shelley had been a summer child. An easy child. She loved the beach and the tides, the sand flats where she could roam. Every new town was an adventure, rooms above Chinese takeaways, caravans on coastal paths and B&Bs that smelled of the seaside. They shared a bed and woke to the sound of the sea. She taught Shelley to swim in the quiet of secret coves. They collected driftwood along the tideline and the deep-pink seaweed that washed in from the coral beds. The seasons came and went but she thinks of Shelley now as a child who grew in the sun.

She walks up the empty high street. The gift shops filled with postcards and sticks of rock are shut on weekdays. The double-decker bus to Bridport roars up the narrow street, leaving a trail of white smoke behind. Blank faces stare back at her through the smeary windows. She'd like to volunteer at the Tenovus charity shop but it's DBS checked. Jimmy says he can speak to them, explain, that they won't turn her away. But she's heard that before and knows that it's like Chinese whispers in a small town like this, her face would be recognised in every shop window. She's had to flatten her accent, develop a monochrome smile. It's a small place to hide.

It's a mile walk to Uplyme, to the Post Office counter in the BP garage that smells of old diesel. It's where she gets the free paper and posts her parcels to Shelley. She found her daughter on Facebook, living above a pub in Derby, as far from the sea as it's possible to get. The woman behind the Post Office counter always weighs the Jiffy bags on her scales. The angular edges of bones and teeth, shells and trace fossils, pieces of the past wrapped in tissue paper.

'Anything valuable?' the woman in the Post Office always asks.

The footpath home follows the river Lim as it cuts through the landscape. She watches the water gurgle and rasp against the rocks, finding its way to the open sea. Some things are unstoppable.

Sometimes she dreams of Shelley, her hair like white

froth, and her sea-blue eyes. Shelley is barefoot, wearing a pale-yellow smock dress with patch pockets. She is a free spirit, climbing over rock pools and wandering along the shoreline with her head bowed. Lulworth beach stretches to the horizon. Shelley is so small she is barely visible. The sea comes in with stealth, like a stalker. Shelley hasn't noticed the water rising as she picks her way amongst the rocks, finding herself stranded somewhere between the sea and the sky. Needing a mother to save her.

The sea does not forget.

Back at the room above the laundrette, there's a note under the door from Mrs Mackay that says her rent is overdue. She's not a woman that will ask twice. It's over a week before her benefits are due. She's offered to help Mrs Mackay with the changeovers, to clean the flats and look after the laundrette, in lieu of rent. But Mrs Mackay says she's already got regular help, that she likes to give jobs to locals. Sometimes it seems as if there's no chance of starting again, no forgiveness.

Jimmy has left three voice messages on her mobile phone and says it's urgent – she needs to ring him back ASAP. Jimmy's voice sounds tight and high-pitched, not like his usual slow-chime conversation. She imagines him scribbling frantically with his pencil in the notebook as he talks too quickly. Jimmy says, 'You know the licence doesn't allow contact with Shelley, for God's sake we've discussed this. What were you thinking?' She can feel her salted eczema scream. She wants to tell Jimmy that a mother can never give up on their children, they will always find a way. Separating her from her daughter has been the crime.

The sea brings the winter high tides to her door.

She walks along the promenade, the sky heavy with winter rain. Out at sea, the wind is rising, tossing the small boats around in the harbour. Sometimes it's hard to ride out a storm. She takes a detour to the beach café and the man stands over her at the counter. His grey-green fossil eyes are observant, looking intently at the name on her bank card, *A. E. Elliot*, as it hovers over the card machine.

'Where you stayin' then?' the man asks.

'Up Monmouth Street,' she says. She drinks her coffee too quickly and it burns the inside of her mouth. Afterwards, the man stares at her through the café window, the flicker of a memory, a news report – something about a child down Lulworth Cove way. His eyes jet dark, retracing her steps.

Sometimes when she swims, she lies prone in the water, her head perfectly still as if she is sleeping. Surrounded by the cold, her limbs feel unconnected to the past. She holds her breath until her lungs hurt. She counts the seconds in her head, marking time. Moving from one town to another, reinventing herself. Maybe it's time to move on, there are always other places to hide. Her life is spent swimming against the tide. Afterwards, her body feels light, as if she might float away.

As a child, no one seemed to care that she stayed out until it was dark, throwing pebbles into the sea and listening to the sound of them sinking. The sky bruised purple, almost black. Her mother shut up in the boxroom at home, always fearing a mudslide or a landslide after another storm. Her mother was as unpredictable as the sea, her moods shifting with the tides. She hadn't ever kept her safe. Sometimes, she wondered if there was another mother on the other side of the ocean. Someone who would carry her home to bed, smooth her hair and sing her to sleep.

She had found Shelley at Lulworth Cove. A small girl alone on the sand, cut off by the tide, the water lapping at her feet. She needed a mother. When she picked the little girl up, she felt as light as driftwood. The watery sky stretched to the horizon. Shelley was cold, her blue lips and chattering teeth. She wasn't wearing enough clothes, she thought. Where was her cardigan? She wrapped Shelley inside her coat, the warm pulse of her breath against her face. The blond froth of her hair was damp and salty. It was only a few steps to the car where they would be warm, the windows steamed up with the fan heater. They drove away, leaving behind the sound of the waves as they pounded the shingle, the sound of raised voices and police sirens. They were in Cornwall in a couple of hours, Shelley tucked up in bed with her. Safe from the sea.

The little girl she saw earlier in the café is on the seafront, running her small hands along the rusty promenade railings. Behind her, her mother is firing words into her mobile phone, vaping and playing with her long hair. The mother hasn't noticed that her little girl is wandering away. Her heart flutters in her chest. The sound of the sea, the waves dragging at the shingle. She asks the little girl if she'd like an ice cream and reaches for her small hand. It fits perfectly inside hers.

She remembers the unpredictable tides, the sea rising and falling. Her daughter Shelley's soft voice on repeat, asking to go home to her mummy. She couldn't let her go.

The sea is anonymous. Forgiving.

The little girl's hand is inside hers and they are walking away. Behind them, the mother has stopped and is still talking on her mobile. She hasn't noticed her daughter edging away. In the distance, she can hear the sound of a siren. On the promenade, footsteps pounding the pavement, the waves crashing onto the shore. She holds tightly onto the little girl's hand; she just wants to keep her safe. It's only a few steps to the car and they can be in Dorset by nightfall. Someone is running after her, shouting, 'Stop.' She doesn't turn round but imagines the man from the café kiosk breathing down her neck, Jimmy waving his notebook and pencil. She scratches at her arms, the sores where the salt water has worked its way into her eczema.

She remembers her mother, her melancholic face. Sometimes, her mother woke up and stared at her as if she didn't even know who she was. She touched her mother's face with the tips of her fingers, ran them around the curve of her lips. She wanted her mother to pick her up and hold her to her chest, to breathe life on her cheek. But her mother's eyes were like the sea, deep and dark. The tide taking her away.

Jimmy has his hand on her arm. His voice is soft, chiming

like a bell. 'It's happening again,' he says. 'Let her go.' She just wants to be loved, she tells him.

# Contributors' Bios

**Melanie Carvalho** is an artist, writer and obituaries editor based in Camberwell, South London. A London Library emerging writer 2022/23, she is currently working on her first novel, *Xim*, which was longlisted for the inaugural Cheshire Novel Prize.

**Jane Copland**'s work has been published in *Witness Magazine*, the *Independent*, *Newsroom*, *Ellipsis Zine*, *JMWW*, *Hayden's Ferry Review*, *trampset*, *Litro Magazine*, *Identity Theory* and other publications. She is a Pushcart Prize and Best of the Net nominee. Jane is from New Zealand and lives in the UK.

**Daniel Draper** is a prize-winning writer from Derbyshire whose work is inspired by folklore and the uncanny of the everyday. His writing has appeared in print, online, and in audio form. If he isn't writing or teaching, he's probably on Twitter @MrDraperMaths.

**Kate Ellis** is a writer based in London. Her short fiction has been published in the *Open Pen Anthology*, *The Mechanics' Institute Review* and *The London Short Story Prize*

*Anthology* among others. In 2020, she was longlisted for the Deborah Rogers Foundation Award for her debut novel. She runs the Brick Lane Bookshop Short Story Prize, hosts the BLB Podcast and works for Inpress Books. Twitter: @katesmalleyelli.

**Samantha Fern**'s work has featured in numerous journals including *The Moth*, *Dear Damsels*, *Loud Coffee Press*, *The Rialto*, *Nightingale & Sparrow*, *Idler*, *Little Stone Journal* and *Dodging the Rain*. She has also appeared in anthologies produced by Dear Damsels, Visual Verse and Arachne Press.

Born and brought up in Mansfield, Nottinghamshire, **Richard Hooton** studied English literature at the University of Wolverhampton before becoming a journalist and communications officer. He has had numerous short stories published and has won prizes or been listed in various competitions. Richard lives in Mossley, near Manchester, and is a member of Mossley Writers.

**Denise Jones**, HonDLitt, FRSA, Freeman of the City of London, studied graphic design, was a primary school teacher and has worked with the bookshop that she co-founded since 1978. She lives in Cable Street and was an elected Labour councillor in Tower Hamlets from 1994 to 2022. Denise strongly supports the arts and is a board member of Rich Mix, Young V&A, Trinity Buoy Wharf Trust and Mulberry Schools Trust. She is Deputy Chair of the Portal Trust, where she chairs the Grants committee, and Chair of the Aldgate & Allhallows Foundation. She has served on the boards of the Arts Council, Museum of London, Whitechapel Art Gallery, Create London, Lee Valley Regional Park Authority and other trusts.

**Helen Kennedy** is a writer of short stories, flash fiction and novels. Her short stories have been published by Fly on the Wall Press in their anthology *The Ones Who Flew the Nest* (2023) and by Retreat West in their anthology *Swan Song* (2023). She has been shortlisted and published by the Bristol Short Story Prize (2022), the Oxford Flash Fiction Prize (2023), Reflex Fiction, Flash 500, and National Flash Fiction Day as part of their New Writer series. She has recently completed a short-story collection, *Acts of Identity Vandalism*, and a novella, *Missing Pieces*. She is currently writing a novel, *Blessed Women*, a love letter to strong Salford women. Instagram: @helenkennedywrites. Email: hkennedy44.hk@gmail.com.

**Sophia Khan** is a primary school teacher and writer from Harrow. She is a member of REWRITE and has been previously published in *REWRITE READS*. She is currently working on a collection of short stories.

**K. Lockwood Jefford** is a Welsh writer and former NHS psychiatrist. Her work has appeared in *Prospect Magazine*, *MIROnline* and many short-story-prize anthologies, e.g. Bristol, Fish, Rhys Davies, *Aesthetica*. She won the V. S. Pritchett Prize (2020), Bath Short Story Award (2021), and 3rd prize, Brick Lane Bookshop Short Story Prize (2020), and recently completed her first collection of short fiction.

**David Micklem** is a writer and theatre producer. He's recently been published by *The London Magazine*, *Litro*,

*STORGY Magazine*, Scratch Books, *The Cardiff Review*, *Lunate*, *bandit* and *Tigershark*, and was shortlisted for the 2022 Bristol Short Story Prize and the 2020 Fish Short Story Prize. His first novel, *The Winter Son*, is seeking a publisher. He lives in Brixton in South London.

**Leeor Ohayon** is a writer from London based in Norwich, where he is pursuing a PhD in creative and critical writing at the University of East Anglia. His work has appeared in *The White Review*, *Prospect*, *Royal Society of Literature Review* and *Paper Brigade*. Leeor was shortlisted for the Brick Lane Bookshop Short Story Prize in 2021.

**Harper Walton** is a writer based in London. They were born in Bath and grew up in the West Country. They studied English literature at Queen Mary University of London and have a master's in creative writing from the Paris School of Arts and Culture. In September 2023 they will start their PhD in English at Royal Holloway, University of London. Their work takes form in prose, poetry, and personal essays.

**Chris Wright** was longlisted for the Irish Book Awards Short Story of the Year, runner-up in the Mairtín Crawford Award, and has featured in many publications, including *A Little Unsteadily into Light* and *Declarations on Freedom for Writers and Readers*. His writing is preserved in the Irish Reading Archive at University College Dublin. Chris has an MA in creative writing from the Seamus Heaney Centre at Queen's University Belfast. He teaches creative writing and is a judge for the Mairtín Crawford Award.

# Judges' Bios

**Melissa Cox** is publishing director for the fiction list at Bonnier Books and was formerly head of books at Waterstones. She's so keen on short stories she once bought a collection she saw someone reading on the Tube based on nothing more than the title.

**Kiya Evans** joined Mushens Entertainment as Juliet Mushens' assistant in 2021. She was promoted to Associate Agent in 2023, and works across Juliet's client list alongside building her own list of authors. After graduating with a BA in history and English from Oxford University, she completed two internships at Mushens Entertainment, and joined as a full-time member of the team in February 2021. You can follow her on Twitter @kiyarosevans.

**Gurnaik Johal** is a writer from West London born in 1998. He won the Galley Beggar Press Short Story Prize 2021/22 and was shortlisted for the *Guardian* 4th Estate BAME Short Story Prize in 2018. He graduated from the University of Manchester in 2019 and works in children's publishing.

# Judges' Quotes

**On the Anthology**

'It's been a pleasure to read such a varied selection of stories, full of different voices, experimentations with language and story-telling and with different approaches to evoking imagery and reaction. The standard was very high and choosing a winner was very difficult – each writer should feel incredibly proud of their work reaching this stage.'

Melissa Cox

'An energising array of short stories, with an abundance of ambition and talent on display. This is a collection in which we found writers taking risks, playing with form, and discovering their voice – an exceptionally gratifying reading experience.'

Kiya Evans

'A formally inventive and consistently surprising patchwork of stories. This wide-ranging collection shows how elastic the short-story form is, and these writers are pulling it in exciting new directions.'

Gurnaik Johal

## 1st Prize

*Kissing in Berlin* by K. Lockwood Jefford

'Rich in detail and sensuality.'

Melissa Cox

'The language is sharp and the dynamic carefully drawn – completely compelling.'

Kiya Evans

'This fraught love story explores an imbalanced relationship from its initial spark to its fuse going off. It's tense, sensuous and bold, as interested in what characters don't see as much as it is in what they do. It's a brilliant story of concealment, of characters taking on different guises to hide themselves or perform different versions of themselves, and of the buttons that hold these guises together coming off.'

Gurnaik Johal

## 2nd Prize

*Lots* by Leeor Ohayon

'Confident, bold writing, a story full of promise.'

Melissa Cox

'Inventive and experimental writing with an assured tone which kept me immersed. I feel like I learned things without the writer trying to "teach" me them.'

Kiya Evans

'Like the Purims it describes, this story is full of sensuality and humour on the surface, with a sense of tragedy and history beneath. The holding together of unruly tangents here creates a bold charge; this story fizzes and sparks like some machine coming apart – and piecing it all together makes for a really enjoyable read.'

Gurnaik Johal

### 3rd Prize

*Oyster Shell Ashtray* by Harper Walton

'An assured piece of writing full of promise.'

Melissa Cox

'Astutely captures the sense of feeling youthful and alive. Fun and intimate and fresh all at the same time.'

Kiya Evans

'This is the kind of story that feels like it has a pulse. It's lively and surprising, written in smooth sharp prose, buzz cut to the scalp. There's a rewarding juxtaposition between our outer appearances and our inner lives.'

Gurnaik Johal

### Shortlisted Stories

*Gybe* by Melanie Carvalho

'An evocative story that captures a moment containing complex feelings.'

Melissa Cox

'Beautiful, contained prose, with strong characterisation lending the reader an immediate understanding of voice and power dynamics.'

Kiya Evans

'A controlled story, locating the personal within the political.'

Gurnaik Johal

*Second-Hand Smoke* by Chris Wright

'An interesting exploration of dark and troubled times through the eyes of young siblings.'

Melissa Cox

'Strikes the balance between childhood voice and adult hindsight very well – the writing is very assured.'

Kiya Evans

'An assured and poised story about something chaotic and unruly. A brilliant handling of a child's point of view in the face of events they can't quite understand.'

Gurnaik Johal

*The Art of Losing* by Samantha Fern

'A powerful and well-observed examination of grief.'

Melissa Cox

'The emotion feels believable and close to the surface. This was an understated but astute depiction of guilt and the writing is very accomplished.'

Kiya Evans

'Emotionally raw and precise on the sentence level, this story renders something so often thought of in hindsight in the present moment.'

Gurnaik Johal

## Longlisted Stories

*A Day at the Beach* by Sophia Khan

'A deft exploration of precarious family dynamics.'

Melissa Cox

'I really enjoyed the family dynamics portrayed here and thought the sense of place was strong.'

Kiya Evans

'A story of oil refusing to mix with water that expertly deconstructs a family unit.'

Gurnaik Johal

*Entanglement* by David Micklem

'Simmers with tension.'

Melissa Cox

'The tension is simmering and threatening, the tone compelling and steady.'

Kiya Evans

'This story finds the high-stakes drama in an inner life, and doesn't pull its punches.'

Gurnaik Johal

*Flight Risk* by Daniel Draper

'An ambitious and imaginative concept to explore a disintegrating relationship.'

Melissa Cox

'An original and ambitious premise.'

Kiya Evans

'You never know where "Flight Risk" is about to turn. It's the kind of short story you feel couldn't be told in another medium.'

Gurnaik Johal

*Ingredients* by Richard Hooton

'I really enjoyed how the writer used food to evoke memories and affection.'

Melissa Cox

'I thought the transitions between food and memories were excellent.'

Kiya Evans

'Sensuous food writing counterbalanced by a sensitive portrayal of two brothers on very different paths.'

Gurnaik Johal

*Just to You* by Jane Copland

'A tense story of workplace harassment.'

Melissa Cox

'A contained and interesting take on a familiar topic.'

Kiya Evans

'A story about the instability of memory which manages to find something new in a plot that is sadly all too familiar.'

Gurnaik Johal

*The Anonymity of a Seaside Town in Winter* by Helen Kennedy

'A deeply, viscerally sinister story.'

Melissa Cox

'The intrigue is subtly and slyly introduced but unfolds in a really compelling way.'

Kiya Evans

'There's something elemental and raw about this story of the sea. Its unsettling tone lingers on after the last page.'

Gurnaik Johal

# Writers' Endorsements

'Writing is often an isolating vocation and winning the Brick Lane Bookshop Short Story Prize gave me validation for my work and allowed me to connect with other writers. I'd recommend it to anyone!'

Imogen Fox, 2022 1st Prize

'Being awarded the third-place prize in the BLB Short Story Prize 2022 had a real impact on my writing life. It was not only a vote of confidence in my writing from a team of judges that I respected and admired, but it also led to me meeting my literary agent, which was a huge step forward in my writing career.'

Emily Gaywood-James, 2022 3rd Prize

'An amazing, affirming experience. It was a completely joyous surprise to have my work read and held carefully by the competition team and the judges. It's such a beautiful feeling to know that people have read your work and somehow connected with it, seen something in it and want to celebrate it.'

Isha Karki, 2019 shortlist

'Writing can feel quite lonesome, strange, insane – so for

me, this competition meant: there's something worthwhile about it. Keep at it, said the announcement. Keep at it, said the book on my shelf. And keep at it, said every response from everyone who read my words. Thanks to the Brick Lane Bookshop Short Story Prize, I keep on keeping at it.'

Kieran Toms, 2020 2nd Prize

'Being awarded 3rd Prize in the 2020 Brick Lane Bookshop Short Story Prize by such a wonderful panel of judges was thrilling and special for me. This prize may be relatively new, but it's already establishing itself as a favourite with short-story writers and readers alike.'

K. Lockwood Jefford, 2020 3rd Prize

'I'll never forget the launch party: my story, with my name, in so many books in so many hands. All because I walked past a poster in the window of Brick Lane Bookshop and thought, "What's the worst that could happen?"'

James Mitchell, 2019 winner

'I think, quite simply, that the BLB Prize made me feel I might not be entirely insane to try and do this writing thing.'

JP Pangilinan-O'Brien, 2021 shortlist

'I was so excited to be shortlisted for the Brick Lane Bookshop Prize 2021 among excellent writers. It's a really great prize that offers all longlisted authors the opportunity to be printed in the Prize anthology and that is an amazing moment in itself – getting to see your words in print.'

Leeor Ohayon, 2021 shortlist

'Entering the Brick Lane Bookshop Short Story Prize was the best thing I did in 2021. I spent so long convincing myself that I wasn't a "real writer" and it is hard to express in words how much being shortlisted in 2021 buoyed my confidence. Seeing my name in print was exhilarating and I got to meet some other lovely and talented writers in the process. I cannot recommend it enough. If you are even slightly considering it, apply! Only good things can come of it.'

Nayela Wickramasuriya, 2021 shortlist

'Being shortlisted gave me confidence in myself and it also led to much bigger things that were out of my control. It was really important.'

Huma Qureshi, 2020 shortlist

'Winning the competition was such a confidence boost. Validation from other writers, editors and agents pushes you to consider your work as valuable and worth the time that you're putting into it. It was such a joy and an honour and I was so grateful to have won it.'

Aoife Inman, 2021 winner

# Thanks

Every writer who submitted a story to the competition.

The fifty long-longlisted writers who made the readers' job so enjoyable and difficult.

The twelve longlisted writers whose excellent stories make up this anthology.

Readers: Xanthi Barker, Maame Blue, Rachel Brook, Ríbh Brownlee, Christina Carè, Emma Cheung, Ralitsa Chorbadzhiyska, Emily Cornell, Ruby Cowling, Andrew Everitt, Natasha Fedorson, Olivia Griffiths, Harriet Hirshman, Bret Johnson, Aysel Dilara Kasap, Liam Konemann, Sarah Lambert, Misha Manani, Stevie Marsden, Jamie McGarry, Kira McPherson, Joe Pilbrow, Lucie Riddell, Max Sydney Smith, Billie Walker, Rhys Wright and Nikita Zankar.

Judges: Melissa Cox, Kiya Evans and Gurnaik Johal.

Denise Jones for her foreword.

Polly Jones for her support.

Rachel Brook and Bret Johnson for their work on social media, research and comms.

Sue Tyley, our invaluable copy-editor and proofreader.

Sophia Pearson for being a constant sounding board.

Our indie bookshop stockists.

Everyone who bought and read the 2019, 2020, 2021 and 2022 anthologies.

Mushens Entertainment for their sponsorship and support, especially Kiya Evans and Juliet Mushens.

Spread the Word for their partnership – special thanks to Bobby Nayyar.

Online listings: writers-online.co.uk, nawe.co.uk, mironline. org, duotrope.com, neonbooks.org.uk, aerogrammestudio. com, christopherfielden.com, pocketmags.com, shortstoryaward. co.uk and nothingintherulebook.com.

Goodreads reviewers.

Clays printers.

Turnaround book distribution, especially Benjamin and Claire.

Brick Lane Bookshop customers for choosing to support an independent.

Brick Lane Bookshop booksellers Denise Jones, Polly Jones, Kalina Dimitrova, Andrew Everitt, Glenn Collins, Bret Johnson, Jo Russell and Rachel Brook, for their hard work keeping the shop so busy and brilliant.

www.bricklanebookshop.org

# BLB Podcast

The BLB Podcast celebrates and interrogates the short-story form. For each episode, we invite a writer to read from and discuss their work. We ask about their writing and editing processes, getting published and what they're reading.

Hosted, produced and edited by Kate Ellis and Peter J. Coles.

Find us at bricklanebookshop.org, or search 'Brick Lane Bookshop' on Spotify, Apple Podcasts or Pocket Casts.

Guests so far:

| | |
|---|---|
| Isha Karki | Vanessa Onwuemezi |
| Aoife Inman | Keith Ridgway |
| Jarred McGinnis | Irenosen Okojie |
| Jem Calder | Manuel Muñoz |
| Wendy Erskine | Gurnaik Johal |
| Leon Craig | Imogen Fox |
| Niamh Mulvey | Jess Walter |
| Huma Qureshi | Eley Williams |
| Ben Pester | |

# BLB Subscription

If you enjoyed this anthology and would like to receive more great books from independent publishers, sign up for Brick Lane Bookshop's Independent Publishing Subscription!

Our subscription service spotlights independent publishers who are making waves in literary fiction and non-fiction. Each month you'll receive a newly released paperback, hand-picked by our booksellers, with a note explaining why we selected it and what we find unique and inspiring about its publisher. Subscribe for three months or more and receive a limited edition Brick Lane Bookshop tote bag.

For more information visit: https://bricklanebookshop. org/subscriptions/